THE ETHOS SERIES

EVOKED

Book One

OLIVIA
MARTINEZ

ISBN: 978-0-578-25675-7

Book Cover by Jess Smith/InkblotsArt
Map by Chaim Holtjer
Interior Book Design by Casey L. Jones — http://www.CaseyBelle.com

CONTENTS

I dedicate this book to readers who, like me, use books as a means of escape. I hope this book may help you find solace—if only for a while.

You are seen.

You are loved.

You are not alone.

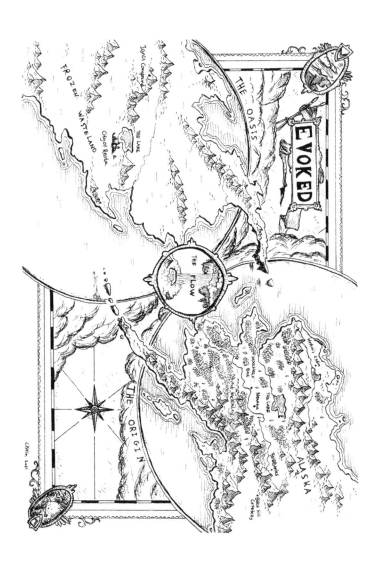

"Even a rock will eventually surrender to the sea, and love can slip away like sand through fingers."

– Michael Faudet

CHAPTER ONE

BYE BYE BIRDIE

VALERIE

MY BROTHER IS DEAD.

The funeral workers spread his casket over a navy cloth while following a How-To for assembling the lowering device. If that strikes you as an unusual practice, you wouldn't be alone since it's meant to be prepared ahead of time—just like you'd expect. But, these workers had what they believed to be a "good idea."

They figured the casket could simply be chucked into the grave since this particular one was empty. They were thrilled at the prospect of a considerable cut to their work-load. My father, on the other hand, wasn't too keen on the idea.

"I will not have four hooligans plop it into the ground like he was some bird in a shoebox!"

Personally, I couldn't care less how the casket found its way into the ground. This wasn't about honoring my dead brother. It wasn't about closure for us, his family.

My father refused to integrate himself into our community and yet continuously made efforts to fit in, which drove him to this spectacle. He went as far as inviting a priest to speak merely because the public expected to see one, though we were far from devout Christians. The "close the blinds, turn off the lights, and act dead should any religious group come a-knocking" kind of far.

To honor this life-long tradition of "blending in" without necessarily being "in," we bought a plot we couldn't afford in a cemetery whose extravagance we couldn't afford only to invite people with whom we weren't allowed to stay connected.

I dug my heel into the cemetery's trademark, and the corner of my mouth pinched into a smirk when it ripped the mesh underneath.

Birch Hill was famous, as far as cemeteries go, for gleaming green all year round. Because in Fairbanks, Alaska, we honored our dead with spray-painted plastic. Global warming was to blame, they said. No amount of fertilizer, even the natural dead body kind, could win a fight against the unyielding snow, so they retired their shovels and introduced acres of phony patches of grass saturated in snows kryptonite—salt. It reminded me of the candy grass concocted by Willy Wonka in his factory, though I imagined it wouldn't taste nearly as good.

My twin brother, Grant, and I stood in the forefront with my father, in his wheelchair, on my right. Behind us, rows of people who didn't belong here. People who, before today, only interacted with us enough as was polite.

Besides Warren Bonhomme, all the other kids from Eren's school knew him as Eren Spencer: the quiet kid with the odd white hair. We assumed his piebaldism hindered his ability to make more friends, but his profound interest in anime and *Pokémon* was also a strong contender. I leaned towards the latter.

The milky white hair never stopped my fraternal twin, who also shared the same rare gene. My guess? On Eren, it rang albino, while on Grant, they deemed it edgy. We three shared our mother's green eyes, but only the boys inherited her mutation, while I, fortunately, received my father's ordinary brown locks. In this unfair game of genetics, only Grant and I came out alive—literally.

But, hair couldn't be enough to fully explain the turn of events.

I had known they picked on Eren at school, but I never imagined it would come to this. A part of me wished that I could've been more attentive. Perhaps, if I had seen the signs, then I could've prevented this.

I could never blame him for what he did. I could only blame myself for not doing my part in lightening his burden. If only I had been more available...

My breath caught in my throat. I didn't want to cry here. I didn't want to hear condolences or feel their sympathy. I wanted to mourn alone. I wanted to yell and curse and throw my lamp across my room without someone telling me it would be okay.

Falling for such a pretense would be the equivalent of believing your parents when they say they sent your dog of fourteen years to live on a farm for the remainder of its life. Does one hope it's true? Of course. But, deep down in your subconscious, you know Fido isn't off chasing chickens out of their coop—and he never will be.

My inability to delude myself made me an emotional ticking time bomb, and I preferred not to take anyone else down with me when I inevitably went off.

"Valerie, you're shaking," Grant whispered, snapping

me back from my thoughts. His hand ran down my arm until it found my own and gave it a tight squeeze. I mustered what I could of a smile and took a deep breath to compose myself.

Father Bethel pulled his cassock over his stocky build to even out the creases and stood at his podium. "My dear friends," he began, "we are gathered here today in memory of Eren Spencer, who was declared dead this past Wednesday after months of searching. I'm inclined to point out that this was the same day the earthquake struck our city. The pain of this decision has resonated through the very earth itself. This was no coincidence but proof. This was the work of Our Lord," he said, glancing at us over his glasses.

I suppressed a scowl. Father Bethel leaped at any opportunity to convert skeptics, but that didn't make a lick of sense.

First, *Our Lord* took my brother from us, and then he ravaged our city? What could I have possibly done to insult Him? Did I forget the Sabbath day? It couldn't be that; I always remembered Sunday. That's when *Game of Thrones* came on.

Father Bethel set off, reciting lines from the book-marked pages in his bible.

I gazed up at the sky and glowered at its unremarkable shade of gray. The sea of clouds looming overhead consumed the sun, so heavy they might fall from the sky and crush us all.

If it would make this day end, I'd welcome them, I thought.

"Life. It can end at any time. So often, there is little we can do about it. Can't plan for it! We may not understand, and we certainly don't have the answers. The casket that will hold your earthly remains might be sitting in a funeral parlor today. Your obituary may be printed next week. Are you prepared?"

"I hope you deleted your internet history," I muttered into Grant's ear.

He laughed and then attempted to mask it with a series of coughs.

I patted his back vigorously to aid his charade, but it wasn't convincing, and our father cast a disapproving look in our direction.

"We must make the most of our opportunities. Do not boast about tomorrow. Today can make a difference, so do what you can today. Help others, serve the Lord, and prepare your souls for eternity. The story of a rich man and Lazarus teaches us life is more than possessions and titles to property. It is not what we have, but what we are," he said, tears welling up in his eyes.

We were still as he let the words settle, but I studied him incredulously. Could anyone genuinely feel that level of sadness over the death of someone they didn't even know? Or was Father Bethel putting on a show?

A sob broke the silence. I turned to see Warren holding his abdomen as he let out another cry. Mrs. Bonhomme threw an arm around him and wiped the tears streaming down his face.

Now, Warren's grief, I could understand. He lost his best friend.

We didn't always need friends. Our mother raised us to depend so much on each other that we were never inclined to form relationships outside of our own family. She sincerely believed blood ran thicker than water and would hammer that into our heads whenever the opportunity arose.

She'd tell us that after she was gone, we were all that

we had left—that we needed to take care of each other. She would tug us along everywhere she went, and we never complained. Those were the most blissful years of our lives. So much so that I've laid in bed and speculated whether they even happened at all.

When Grant and I were thirteen and Eren only four, our parents were in a car accident. We waited for them to leave that morning with a swelling sense of rebellion, an emotion we seldom got to feel since we had never been left alone before. We watched horror movies and ate sweets to our heart's content, things we could never do with our mother watching over us like a hawk. Little did we know we'd have the rest of our lives to do so.

That night, the police came knocking on our door to break the news. Soberly, they informed us of our father's severe injuries and the medical examiner's pronouncement of our mother's death at the scene. My father lost all sensation below the waist and his usual zest for life, which he buried along with his wife, forcing him to quit his forester job to care for us. We had to make do with what little he received of disability after exhausting our savings.

Grant and I relied on each other for the first few months, given that we shared the same age and maturity, which left four-year-old Eren to roam around the house looking for her—too young to understand that he'd never see her again. We didn't appreciate being reminded of that fact, so we'd tell him that she was in a better place and to simply let it go while gradually, unbeknownst to us, creating deep fractures in our relationship. Which, in turn, forced Eren to outsource for emotional companionship.

Of course, we thought nothing of it at the time— except perhaps relief that he had quit raising the subject. We never spoke of my mother again, too afraid to reopen

old wounds. Now, in retrospect, I could admit how undeniably selfish we had been.

"There are two things we cannot escape: death and
judgment. So let us use our time wisely in preparing,"
Father Bethel said, signaling the end of the service.

We listened to the motorized hum of the device as it
cranked the casket into the ground until, at last, it reached
its final destination, and the workers began to loosely
shovel dirt over the empty box.

I glanced down at my father. He wore his only suit and
tie—the same suit he wore to his wedding, his wife's
funeral, and now, the same suit he wore to his sons.

My father clutched his thighs, his veins protruding from
his aged hands as he watched. I never thought I'd say it,
but it was a good thing he couldn't feel his legs.

Father Bethel stepped down from the podium, and the
people around us began to disperse.

"I'll take Dad," Grant said. "You coming?"

I hesitated. I couldn't tell my brother how the idea of
leaving the cemetery, the finality of it, had me paralyzed.
My guilt made it impossible to move, but Grant coped by
running. He ran away from anything remotely challenging
to distance himself from the harsh reality. Of course,
Grant attended Eren's funeral. They were brothers, after
all, and he wasn't wholly heartless. Still, I knew we had
limited time with him now.

Eren and I became undeniably close when Grant
distanced himself. He forgave me for abandoning him
while I relied on Grant and stepped up to the challenge
whenever I came to him with issues he couldn't yet understand, like when Derek Yates cheated on me during my
freshman year of high school.

During Eren's Girls-Are-Yucky stage, I ran home in

tears, a blubbering mess, and the only two discernible words out of my mouth were "Derek" and "asshole." He obviously had no experience dealing with asshole Derek's, so he did all he could do. He sat with me and told me I was too pretty for him. Though only six years old then, he already understood how to perk a girl up.

With Eren gone and my father mentally checking out years ago, Grant was the only person on the planet who could possibly comfort me now, so I had to play it cool. He couldn't know what this did to me. He couldn't handle Mom passing; he wouldn't stay for this. If I showed any sign of weakness, it would make this real for him. But having Grant back felt like an endless audition for a play whose role I had already lost.

Even so, I couldn't move. Not just yet.

"Are you crazy?" I asked, motioning towards the shoveling men. "They need supervision. Heard Scruffy over there asking how much the coffin might go for on the black market."

Grant raised a brow. "Good luck with the surveillance. Dad's been eyeing me to rescue him from Mrs. Weisman. I better wheel him away before he rolls himself into the grave, too," he said and sauntered off.

The men finished moments later and bowed their heads to me before leaving.

Now alone, I knelt on the newly turned earth. Engraved on the slab of stone, "Eren Spencer. May eleventh, nineteen-ninety-eight—September twenty-fourth, twenty-fifteen. Your memory lives on."

I kept trying, yet failing, to piece the fragments of evidence together.

There was a lake. A deep black lake that somehow hadn't frozen over after months of thirty-ish degree weather. Something the authorities were "looking into." A bridge crossed over this lake, one that my father told the officers he must have jumped from after they ruled out foul play.

The lead investigator declared suicide the only viable option after my father told her about Eren's note found in his room. He refused to tell us exactly what it said, only that it gave them enough information to lead them there and to believe any injuries found on him were likely to be self-inflicted.

Its waters were deep, and my brother didn't know how to swim. Not a lot of people in Alaska do. An empty bottle of Zoloft prescribed to Enki Spencer, my father, bobbed in the water. My father left the body unattended to call for help, only for the body to vanish when the help finally arrived.

After searching every fissure of the lake, they organized a search party to comb the woods surrounding it. A month's worth of time and resources later, they concluded the body had either been consumed by one of the lake's inhabitants or drifted off to the shore, where opportunistic scavengers in the woods had a field day. So basically, their theory revolved around creatures gorging on my brother. Lovely.

That story had been fed to me countless times, but I couldn't seem to swallow it—pun intended. Perhaps because part of me still hoped it was just a huge misunderstanding.

I had hoped Eren spontaneously left to some comic book convention, too afraid to tell us and be the butt of Grant's male chauvinistic jokes, but somehow got stranded. I could almost see him lining up at the *Samurai Champloo* booth or taking selfies with a group dressed as characters from *Attack on Titan*.

Except he was cautious and good-natured. Unlike

Grant and I, the mutinous twins, Eren wouldn't move an inch without asking for permission first. And he wouldn't leave Warren behind. This theory proved challenging to keep alive, but I managed.

I had hoped my father jumped to conclusions and mistook his body for a branch or maybe even a bear. Bear carcasses were familiar sights in the area due to lazy or overzealous hunters, shocking as it may seem. Safe to assume my father needed some sort of closure and imagined it all.

Except my father was the most level-headed and reliable man I knew. He would never accept his son had passed on unless he saw it with his own eyes and, although I could never bring myself to ask, I knew he would've made sure. He would've made *damn* sure.

I let my hands sink into the softened dirt, closed them into fists, and shut my eyes while my heart twisted into unusual shapes in my chest. I took a deep breath and imagined what Eren would do if he were here.

He would kneel beside me and take my hand, not saying a word. He wasn't much for them. His hand in mine would have been enough, but there's no relief for me now.

My eyes stung as tears fell to the ground, remembering the shy smile Eren would don when I'd compliment his drawings, and the warm laughter I'd hear when I'd whine over losing against him in a video game. All the little things that I took for granted.

I sank deeper into my thoughts until a low crackling sound caught my attention. I opened my eyes and squealed, recoiling from what appeared to be working its way up to the surface.

A blade of grass grew swiftly from underneath the freshly shoveled dirt. I was no botanist, but my faint recollection of the *Planet Earth* documentary I'd seen made me uneasy at the rate it sprouted. It resembled the show a little *too* much. The growth shown in the documentary had been filmed over several days, while this happened within seconds. How was this possible?

Then louder snapping sounds, this time by the tombstone where long stems rose from the earth, crawling up its sides. Vines!

As they made their way to the top, they reached for those around them for support, coiled, and then released further upward in a captivating dance of twirling green. I watched in awe as the tombstone became covered in them. I held one of the tiny tendrils, and as soon as my fingers made contact, a small white flower bloomed on its tip.

"Valerie!"

I dropped the vine and hurried to my feet. I brushed the dirt from my hands onto my dress as a bizarre feeling washed over me—a sudden impulse to hide the plants, as though I had been caught doing something I shouldn't be doing. As though I were being watched.

A woman, who looked to be in her mid-forties, stood by an eerie angel statue a few yards away. When our eyes met, hers narrowed. She stared at me as if I were a walking Rubik's cube, head tilting and all. Then, she moved towards me, tucking a strand of umber hair behind her ear.

"Uh, hello! Earth to Valerie!" Grant's voice boomed, his arms waving over his head.

She stopped in her tracks and shifted her gaze in his direction—the V between her eyes growing more pronounced. If she were to have noticed how weird Mother Nature acted a moment ago, her head would explode.

I took one last glance at Eren's plot before catching up to Grant.

I could no longer see the cheerless gray of the tombstone but a vibrant green. Only the engravings remained exposed. And, what was once only dirt now brimmed with blades of grass, a shade of green I had never seen here in Fairbanks.

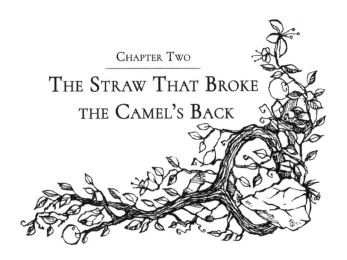

CHAPTER TWO

THE STRAW THAT BROKE
THE CAMEL'S BACK

THE RECENT EARTHQUAKE LEFT OUR ROADS UNFIT TO drive, so we walked, with Father Bethel leading the way. Our guests didn't venture ahead of us. They wouldn't want to come across as overly anxious to get home—when they were. No one spoke at first, but after a few minutes of silence, the peace came to an end.

An old, wrinkly retiree with an even older set of values, Margaret Crowley, made her way through the crowd. She smiled a little too brightly at us and walked in stride with Father Bethel.

"Oh, what a horrible tragedy this is. I can hardly believe it," Margaret said.

"The boy is in a better place," Father Bethel replied.

"Taking his own life and just when he was in his prime!"

"It is a tragedy at any age."

I wasn't sure whether priests were allowed to dislike fellow Christians, but if they could, then Father Bethel and I would officially have one thing in common.

"The words of Our Lord need to be particularly read to our children," she said. "If he had gone to church more often, then maybe this tragedy could have been prevented. After all, if you forsake the Lord, then he shall forsake you."

I stopped in my tracks. Mr. Lindat, the owner of the town's only bookstore my brother frequented, didn't notice and walked right into me.

"Valerie . . ." my father cautioned. By his tone, he knew what was going to happen next.

Crowley didn't, and so she continued. "It was rather selfish of him if you ask me."

"Well, no one's asked you," I snapped.

We had stopped walking. Crowley turned in my direction, and the crowd followed suit.

"That's enough of that. Let's get back to the house," my father urged, smiling apologetically at the now very insulted old woman.

I had always known she wasn't fond of my family. As the woman in charge of the local church events, she noted how we didn't participate in any community functions and never set foot in the church. She quite possibly assumed we were Satanists.

If it meant she'd leave us alone, I would've converted in a heartbeat, but alas, here she was.

"Such uncouth manners from such young a lady," Crowley said. "You speak when you are spoken to, child."

I laughed. It wasn't the best day to pick a fight with me. "With Alzheimer's looming over you," I began, "I know this may be a bit fuzzy, but in this day and age, I could damn well say what I want when I want."

She shook her bony finger in my face. "You are mistaken. Your mother shouldn't have filled your heads with all this free spirit nonsense when she was still springing about. Not your fault, but also not mine, so when you are in my presence, you will speak to me as though your mother taught you some manners to go with that pretty face."

Grant tensed, muttering something exceedingly impolite under his breath, but proceeded to place his hand on my back in an attempt to steer me away.

But my blood was boiling. It was one thing to insult me, but to insult my dead brother and mother was a whole other story.

Oh no, I thought. *If it's a show Crowley wants, then I'll give her one.*

My father's expression warned me not to respond, but it was too late, and I could be ignorant of social cues when I wanted to.

"No, no, she's right!" I laughed, looking straight into the hags' beady eyes. "I'll be sure to ask her the next time I visit her grave. Then do you know what I'll do? I'll stroll down to your mother's and ask why she didn't use a wire hanger to abort you when she had the chance." I then added "bitch" a second later for color.

I had detonated. The words were out before I could stop them. Everyone gasped behind me, and if I were to look, stunned faces would be plastered on each and every one of them, so I didn't. Instead, I chose to watch Crowley's as it changed from one emotion to the next: surprise, outrage, revulsion, and finally, pure unadulterated loathing.

"Go," my father ordered, slamming his fist onto the arm of his wheelchair. "*Now!*"

I shot her one last look and fabricated a smile. "I'd apologize, but I seem to lack the manners to do so."

I walked off as conversations erupted in my wake, and I took that as my round of applause.

Though we were only a few yards away from my home, I was impatient to get back, so I jogged and heard someone's running steps and ragged huffs behind me.

"Hey," Warren breathed.

"Hey." I could tell he wanted to say more, though he couldn't catch his breath long enough to say it. Of course, the polite thing to do would be to slow down, but I wasn't worried about being polite anymore. That ship had long since sailed.

Naturally, the earthquake hit my block the hardest, completely shattering the road, so I had to lift my legs higher with each stride to avoid the serrated edges of concrete. Warren just barely kept up.

By the time we reached my doorstep, we were winded. Running could be hazardous in the harsh Alaskan weather. I pressed my back against the door for support and got very little. I might as well have leaned on a block of ice for all the good it did.

Warren stood in front of me and put his hands on his knees, wheezing, and it brought to mind Eren's incessant teasing about an alleged crush Warren had on me, and now I couldn't shake the thought away. Warren was too thin for his height—lanky. His eyes were red from the funeral, and his nose a bright pink from the run. His thick curly hair that stuck out from underneath his winter cap and thin chapped lips made him look younger than nineteen. It would be beyond awkward if true, seeing as I had seven years on the kid.

"I was just—I was wondering if you were okay."

I stared at him. My breathing had returned to normal. His hadn't.

He shook his head, his hand forming an explosion by

his temple. "Obviously, you're not okay. We just left Eren's funeral. What I meant to say—"

"I'm fine."

"Good." He smiled briefly before patting his pockets and retrieving an inhaler. He then placed his lips to the mouthpiece and took a deep, slow pull.

Right, he had asthma. Shit. I should have slowed. The polite thing to do now would be to invite him inside and apologize for being a shitty human being, but all I wanted to do was contemplate my shitty-ness in the privacy of my room.

"Look, I'm sorry. It's been a long day, and I kind of want to be alone right now. Can we talk some other time?" I asked, but it felt lacking. "Tomorrow?" I offered, worried he'd feel as though I were throwing him out, even though I was.

He straightened himself while attempting to fix his cap but pulled it too far back, only for it to glide right off. "That sounds like a great, amazing idea. Yeah. Maybe grab some coffee? I would totally be up for that if that's what you want."

"Sure," I said. Boy, was I going to regret this.

He shot me a big boyish smile and backed away, his eyes never leaving mine. Then, after a few seconds of gauche eye contact, he forgot the number of steps leading up to the porch and fell gracelessly onto his back.

Yep. Eren was right.

I rushed forward to help, but he got up faster than he fell. He gave me one last nervous smile and waved before running off.

I waved back, wondering how he could be so clumsy and I so damn cruel.

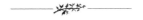

THE FOLLOWING DAY, I WOKE UP TO THE SOUND OF THE television in the living room. I lumbered groggily to the bathroom, rubbing the sleep from my eyes.

I had made a deal with myself last night that I could cry as much as I'd like so long as I avoided mirrors the next day. So, I mentally tallied every hurtful thing I had ever done or said to Eren and bawled my eyes out, counting on the fact that I wouldn't see the damage, but I caught my reflection in the mirror and groaned.

I was *The Blob*. My face had puffed up double its size while I slept, and my eyes were nearly impossible to see over the shadow of my swollen lids. I made a mental note never to do all my crying in one night—if not for my sake, then for my family's. They had suffered enough.

I declared it too dangerous to comb through the bird's nest on my head, so I popped into the shower. And I had to be honest with myself; they would never cast me as Chewbacca in the new *Star Wars* film, though I resembled Chewie more than Chewie himself right now, so I shaved my legs before stepping out of the shower, into a towel, and onto my bed.

I didn't want to think anymore, and I became disturbingly good at doing just that. The key was to imagine myself as an empty shell—devoid of all reason or emotion. I found this disconcertingly easy to do, but again, I pushed that thought out right along with the rest of them.

I sat for a long time doing a swell job at voiding (the term I had officially coined for it) when my stomach growled. I didn't have the energy to rummage through my closet to find something to wear, so I shimmied into the same black dress and stockings I had worn to the funeral. With dirt still smeared on it from the day before, it fit my mood. What did it matter, anyway?

My father was in the living room watching some show

about drug cartels. The cold had begun to creep in through our thin walls, so I glanced around for our quilt only to notice it neatly folded over Grant's pillow on the couch. I fluffed it up before draping the quilt over my father's shoulders, listening out for any hint of Grant's whereabouts.

"Morning," I said.

My father didn't look away from the television but patted my hand softly. "Morning, sweetheart."

When the show went to a commercial break, panic surged through me. A woman listed off the numerous side effects for Prozac in an inconsiderately chipper tone, including none other than "suicidal thoughts and behaviors." It wasn't Zoloft, but it was close enough.

I dove towards the remote and changed the channel. Though hearing the words nearly made me sick, my father appeared unfazed. Crisis averted, I guess?

I caught a whiff of fish and garlic wafting from the kitchen and remembered we were given a tuna casserole during the wake. I strode into the kitchen under the guise of serving myself a plate and took a tiny breath to quell my relief when I saw Grant digging into that same dish straight out of the pan.

"How is it?" I asked, becoming more animated as I took him in.

"It tastes better than it did yesterday," he said. "Why tuna, though? It's not really the sort of thing anyone would want to eat the day after a funeral... Whatever happened to the standard mac and cheese?"

"Was it Crowley's submission?" I asked, scanning the area around the pan for a note that might tell me. "Because, if it was, then I wish I hadn't held back. Anyone that makes you heat up fish in the morning is just plain evil. The house is going to smell like this all day."

"You *didn't* hold back," he laughed. "But, I agree. Mac and cheese, folks. If it ain't broke, don't fix it."

Though the cook had been a tad heavy-handed with the garlic and cooked the pasta for far too long, we were in no condition to whip something up ourselves. So, we stood in silence, taking turns forking bits of it into our mouths. It was sort of peaceful until Grant had to go and ruin it by announcing he had to go.

"But you're coming back, right?"

He shook his head, feigning to struggle with scooping the last remaining morsel of tuna so he could avoid my eyes.

I knew this would happen. Grant found me tolerable to be around when life was easy, but not so much when things were tough, apparently. But so soon?

I assumed I had prepared for it, but my chest tightened. Grant planned to abandon me again, leaving me to deal with this alone, and I didn't know if I could.

I seized the now-empty pan and turned to wash it in the sink, hoping he didn't notice my reaction. "If you have to," I said.

He wrapped his arms around me, pulling me into a deep hug from behind.

After a few seconds of stiffness, I loosened up and accepted it.

I understood we all managed pain differently. While I craved the companionship of those I loved who could understand my pain, Grant preferred to place his in a box and throw away the key. With that being said, only one of us could get what we needed.

"Take care of Dad," he said, pulling away.

"Of course," I muttered. "Someone has to."

I expected Grant would see that as a challenge or at the

very least try to defend himself. But, instead, he sighed and left.

IT HAD BEEN A FEW HOURS SINCE GRANT TOOK OFF, AND I had finally gotten around to doing laundry. A menial task, but it kept my mind and hands relatively occupied.

"I need you to take me somewhere."

I jumped. I hadn't heard my father come in over the violent tumbling of our ancient drying machine. "And where is that?"

"I'll give you the directions as we go," he said, scratching his head. "I need to show you something."

I shrugged. I could use the distraction.

CHAPTER THREE

DOWN THE RABBIT HOLE

THAT SOMETHING HAPPENED TO BE THE INFAMOUS LAKE— not exactly the distraction I anticipated. And it was *filthy*. Its waters reached a point past murky, almost as though it had been drained and loaded with black ink, and I understood why someone had thought to construct a bridge above it, though it had seen better days.

I listened to the faint lapping of water as it carried rotten vegetation to the shoreline with a growing sense of discomfort. How had Eren stumbled upon this place?

My father motioned for me to take us to the decrepit bridge.

"What the fuck, Dad?"

"Please," he insisted.

I led us there reluctantly, but once at the top, I crossed my arms and shot my father a dubious look, trying to ignore the shiver running down my spine.

There was something eerie about the stillness of the lake and surrounding woods. I mean, shouldn't we be able to hear rustling in the bushes or birds singing in the trees?

No toads croaked, and no insects buzzed over the wind's ominous whispering through the trees, either—no sign of life.

My father chuckled, his head leaning against his hand. "I don't know what I'm going to do with you, Valerie."

My arms dropped to my sides. Though my father laughed, I could sense something bubbling underneath, something more.

"When I brought him here—"

"*You* brought Eren here?" The inky lake's fishing potential was lost on me.

He nodded, looking at the water, and continued where he left off. "There were no hassles. He was quiet, probably wondering the same things as you, but he didn't voice them. Just happy to be out with me. But with you," he said, raising a brow, "it won't be so easy."

"What are you talking about?" I wanted to get out of here so badly, and then it hit me again. The police never recovered Eren's body. I closed my eyes and nearly gagged, only for my father's weeping to bring me back.

"I miss him, Val. I miss him so much, and I don't know if I'll ever see him again."

That's all it took. I cried, and I couldn't jot these tears away—more would follow. I knelt down to face my father in his chair and held his hands in mine.

"I miss him too," I said, holding onto him as tight as I could, as though my hands were enough to keep him from falling apart.

"I'm losing everything. There was never a point to any of it," my father cried, his mouth quivering with emotions he couldn't contain. "I can't survive this much longer." His eyes were wide as though they searched for answers to whatever questions thrashed around in his head. I had never seen him so upset, so…defeated.

"No, Dad, please," I begged. The look of sheer help-lessness had me on edge. "You are *everything* to us."

He let out a sob. "Your mother should have been the one to raise you, not me," he said, his head hanging in defeat. "I don't know what I'm doing."

"No!" I squeezed his hands tighter, anger welling up inside me. "You did everything you could, okay? We owe everything we are to you," I said as firmly as I could. My eyes searched for his until I found them. "What Eren did, it had nothing to do with us. He loved us. He loved you. And I love you. Please, don't think this way."

He freed his hand and placed it on my cheek. "You are so precious. You are unlike anything I've ever seen."

I laughed through my tears, holding his hand to my cheek. "I'm all you, Dad."

A shadow crossed his face. "No," he said. "You have your mother's eyes."

Before I could decipher his bizarre expression, some-thing grabbed ahold of my ankle and jerked me away from him and onto my stomach, making my face hit the dock with a loud thud.

My father's hand slipped out of mine, and I screamed. I fought to find leverage on the wooden planks as the fric-tion of the wood scraping against my skin brought fresh tears to my eyes. I called out to my father, begging him for help, but he only sat with his face in his hands.

Why won't he do something?

I had reached the border of the bridge, and I could hear the water splashing. My only hope would be to latch onto the ledge and pull myself up and away from whatever tried to drag me under. I readied myself, but just as I went to grip the ridge, I got viciously yanked back.

I didn't have time. The bridge grew further and further away until whatever had a hold on my ankle plunged me into the water, and, instantly, my skin *burned*. The water, it had to be something with the water.

I needed to free my leg, but I had been dipped into a pool of acid. I was on *fire*. I tried to twist free, but its hold only tightened as I struggled. I had to concentrate. Soon, I wouldn't just be on fire. I'd be out of oxygen.

I opened my eyes, and my hands covered them immediately. Stupid, stupid, stupid. My eyes caught the flame. I wouldn't have been able to see through the filth, anyway, and now it felt like someone had squirt lemon right into my eyes. I shut them as hard as I could and tried not to think about the pain.

I couldn't let this thing drag me down any further. I moved towards my leg and felt my way down until my hands touched something rigid and textured. I fought the instinct to flinch away and gripped it. I tried to pry it off, but something else circled around my wrist and pulled it back.

And that was it. I was out of air. I kicked and pulled, but it was hopeless. Finally, my lungs couldn't take it anymore. I took a deep, desperate breath but found water, and now, what burned my skin had found its way into my lungs. The heat radiated from my chest, but there was nothing more I could do. I couldn't breathe.

Something wrapped itself around my waist, but I'd lost all the energy to fight. So I allowed it to pull me under and only vaguely registered when we reached the bottom.

THE SEARING HEAT EMANATING FROM MY CORE ROUSED ME.

My feet pushed against the lakebed for momentum, shooting me upwards, and this time, nothing held me down. My strokes and kicks were frantic. My mind focused on only one thing: oxygen.

I broke through the surface, heaved the water out of my airways, and gasped. My lungs rejoiced. I forgot the rest of my body's agony for a brief moment and took deep, aiding breaths. My lungs expanded and contracted almost simultaneously.

Once my body replenished its oxygen supply, it focused on getting out of the lake, which had my nerves going haywire. I searched for the shore only to swivel in place.

Everything was just going too well for me. I had begun to hallucinate.

My father, the bridge, the trees, everything had vanished. The sun continued to glow weakly above, but everything else had disappeared, and now ice surrounded me on every side.

A few yards away, the black ink met a white glistening shore. A wall of ice nearly three stories tall stood ahead and looked to go on for miles. Behind me, a frozen wasteland.

Though I was sure it was all in my head, I couldn't stay in the lake until my mind snapped back to reality, so I took my chances with the wall and swam towards it. As soon as my feet touched the ground, I dashed through the water and threw myself onto the bed of snow, encasing myself in it. But, just as my body rid itself of the heat, the cold seeped in ever more quickly. I got to my feet, only to hear voices approaching from behind the wall, startling me.

My dad's called for help, I thought, and relief washed over me. *The nightmare's over*.

"I'm here!" I called out to them.

The voices stopped.

I stumbled towards the wall and tapped on the ice. "I think I may have a concussion," I said, recalling my head slamming against the bridge earlier—the only logical explanation for my hallucinations.

One of them hissed something to the other only to be hushed before he could finish his thought. Something about their brief interaction was off. And, though I couldn't quite point out why exactly, I knew my father was not among them.

I crouched down in the snow, hoping it wasn't too late. I strained to quiet my breathing, but the snow underfoot gave way, and I couldn't help but groan. I had fallen into a ditch, the impact making my knees buckle. Snow began to cover the opening, so I raised my arms over my head to shield myself from the falling snow, but it never came. It formed on every side, confining me.

Hysterically, I clawed at it, but no matter how much I tried, my fingers couldn't pierce through the dense snow. My breathing turned ragged, and my heart stammered in my chest as panic began to seep in. I stood trapped in a snow coffin with no conceivable way of escaping.

Then, my body lurched forward as if I'd been standing in a bus as it came to an abrupt stop. But I hadn't moved. I couldn't have moved.

My entire frame shook—my nose, ears, and fingers were numb. Not even in Alaska did the temperature reach this low, and it stumped my body. First, it had to endure the acidic lake and now the icy snow.

I wondered fleetingly which was worse, but hands down, the acid took the cake.

I lurched forward yet again, but this time the snow around me dissipated, falling at my sides, allowing the dim sunlight to seep through an opening—which appeared to be fifteen feet above me now.

It looked as though I had fallen into an empty well with walls so smooth and glossy they looked like glass, though they were too cloudy to see through. But, as I glimpsed above me, this was the least of my worries.

By the rim of the opening were two colossal men almost indistinguishable apart from a nasty scar one had on his throat. Squinting to get a better look, I noticed they both sported strange blue-tinted hair buzzed short and skintight steely wetsuits that clung to their built frames. They watched me with calculated expressions.

"Who are you?" Scar asked, his deep voice resounding off the ice walls.

"Valerie," I answered. "I'm not sure what's happened, but I got dragged into a lake, and somehow . . . fell. Could you help me out of here?" I asked, crossing my arms as I fought to keep the cold at bay.

"What are you?" the other asked.

"*What* am I?"

"Answer the question."

I shook my head, unable to discern what he asked of me. "It would be easier if we could talk once you've pulled me out," I said, wiping the trickles of blood oozing down my forehead.

They stared at me for a few seconds before walking out of view.

"Hello?!" I called out.

Though they didn't answer, I could faintly hear them whispering to each other.

"Did you get a look at her eyes? I must be imagining this."

Someone sighed. "No, I noticed the color too."

"But that would mean—"

"We need to find Calder. Fast. We need to answer that question ourselves rather than wait for her to show us."

And then, silence. I called out for the men again but to

no avail. Something was wrong. They weren't going to pull me out of here.

I was stuck in this hole, with my only way of escaping towering overhead. I stretched the sleeves of my dress over my hands, rubbing them together, but it did little to warm me. I was still drenched from the lake. I paced the small space trying to find reason within the unreasonable but came up with zilch.

Frantically, I searched for something around me, anything that could possibly be of some use, only to notice vertical white lines covering the walls.

I took an involuntary step back.

Someone had been here before me, and from the look of the marks all around me, they were here long enough to attempt to claw themselves out. An action so obviously futile, it only meant they felt they had no other choice.

I staggered away from the claw marks until I felt the wall and sunk to the ground, tears welling up in my eyes. I didn't know where I was, but it seemed as though I would get to know the place.

Chapter Four

The Lion's Den

A violent rattling woke me, and it took me a while to remember where I was. It turned out the rattling, which made my teeth chatter, came from me. The blood that previously trickled down my forehead was now dry and cracked when I frowned. I had no idea how much time had passed, but the opening above appeared darker.

I heard voices creeping up. I recognized them as those of the brothers who had found me earlier, and it sounded as though they were describing that exact sequence of events to someone else.

Then, a man peered down at me. At first, I thought it might've been one of the two men from before since he had the same strange blue-tinted hair and eyes, but this man was much older, his features more severe. His expression, a mix between curiosity and disgust, surprised me. I shuddered, completely taken aback by it.

"Girl, describe your parents to me," he said, his tone brisk and to the point.

Whatever I expected him to say, it was not that. I must've misheard. "My parents?"

"What would you say are their defining features?"

"I . . . I don't know. I wouldn't say my parents have any."

"What color are your father's eyes and hair?" he asked.

"Brown."

He nodded. "And your mother's?"

I began only to stop myself. I almost mentioned my mother's milky white hair, but a sudden urge to omit that particular tidbit of information overwhelmed me. So instead, I told him she had brown hair and green eyes to account for mine. I was only half lying, anyway.

"Interesting," he said. He smiled, but it wasn't kind— far from it. "I noticed you said, 'had.' Is your mother dead?"

I nodded.

He moved away from view, but I heard him say, "I don't believe she knows. Otherwise, she would have threatened us by now."

"We can't take that chance," one of the brothers complained.

"How do you hide an impure child in our world?"

"You can't."

"No, you can't," the older man agreed. "Her father must've raised her away from the Natura. Laec, have Pavati check our records for any Ventus marked for treason around the time she was born—I'd say around twenty-five or so years ago. There couldn't have been many. And Salil, I need you to find Nerio so he can work on her. If she lied about her mother, there might be more she's neglecting to tell us."

"With all due respect, Calder. I'm done playing second fiddle to that urchin. I am more than capable—"

"Enough," Calder demanded. He was in charge, no question about it. "Like you said, we can't take any chances."

And then, they were gone.

There was a lot to unpack here. How did Calder know that I lied about my mother's hair color? Why would it be significant to them, anyhow? There were freak genetic anomalies of that sort everywhere if you were to really pay attention. But then, why did I hesitate to admit hers? And who were these Natura and Ventus he mentioned? What the hell was going on here?

Though I had ample time to contemplate this, I was nowhere near an answer when I heard footsteps approaching again.

A bald-headed man with a prominent blue beard peered over the edge of the hole. I found it bizarre how they all seemed to share the same enthusiasm for that specific color. Real original.

"The name's Nerio, and I'll be your guide for this evening," the man purred before laughing at his own joke. His raspy voice placed emphasis on unusual syllables when he spoke. "First on our agenda, I'll need you to tell me the location of your father."

I eyed him defiantly. "No."

"I suggest you take a look around and reconsider." He waited for my response, and when it didn't come, he stretched his arms out, his palms open to face me, and from them, a stream of dark water gushed out.

I sprung back against the wall to avoid it, but with nowhere to go, the water hit me smack in the face, and a blood-curdling scream erupted from my throat the second it made contact with my skin. It burned just like the lake did. And just like the lake, the *unbearable* pain that ensued made me frantic, leaving my entire nervous system in shambles. I rubbed my face to try to soothe myself but only made the feeling spread to my hands, making me fall onto my knees and into a pool of even more of the stuff. I couldn't escape it.

"Please, please," I begged. I couldn't go through this again. I clawed at the walls of the ice tomb, searching for a crevice I could use to boost myself up.

Nerio yelled something at me before opening his palms and dumping more of the lake water into the hole until it was knee-deep. I scarcely heard him repeat his demand over my frantic screams.

"Someone . . . please . . . help!" I yelled, the words fraying my throat raw.

I clawed at the walls and screamed for what felt like hours until my lungs could no longer bear it, and I doubled over, expelling any remnants of food I still had in my system.

After the episode, I collapsed into the water and scrambled to get back on my feet. The pain was almost indescribable, and yet with my fatigue, I couldn't lift myself up. So I knelt instead, sobbing into the pool of vomit and acid, as I braced myself for the next wave.

When it didn't come, I peered up through the gap between my arms, only to notice Nerio had gone.

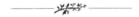

HOURS TICKED BY, WITH THE PAIN NEVER SUBSIDING. THE rancid water made my nostrils sting with every intake of breath since I had nowhere else to relieve myself, and my vomit had been festering on its surface for days. I chose to breathe from my mouth instead, though now I could somehow taste it in the air, too—only exacerbating the ickiness in my mouth.

The ongoing burning sensation from the acid made my muscles twitch uncontrollably around the clock, but I barely noticed anymore. I had grown accustomed to it. The twitching, never the pain. I kept searching my skin for any sign of chemical burns, but every inch I examined came up clear. What sort of acid burns your nervous system while leaving your clothes and skin intact?

I waded in the water, trying to stay in motion to avoid the floating patches of vomit. Then, hoping it would distract me, I resorted to biting my nails—an unpleasant habit I hadn't done since my mother died. It did nothing to ease the agony brought on by the acid, but it was something to do.

Nerio returned over the next couple of days, always with the same questions: where is your father? Do you have any siblings that look like you? All basic questions, and I refused to answer them all. He could have asked me what my favorite color was, and I still wouldn't tell him. I couldn't give the man any piece of factual information, knowing what he was capable of. I couldn't allow my father, or anyone for that matter, to suffer the same fate.

Calder would show up occasionally to watch the inter-action between his henchman and me, and though he usually remained stoic, he'd sometimes shake his head at something I said. I grew tired of trying to decipher why and purposefully ignored him when he showed.

Yet another blue-haired person, who called herself Pavati, came to visit me. She lowered my daily meal to me on a tray tied to a rope and waited while I ate. It wasn't much—bread, frothy flavorless soup, and a glass of water. She became my only respite and sense of time; how I'd know when a full day had passed.

At first, I'd have at it. I would devour it in minutes. Then, on the seventh day, I figured it would be pointless to eat if I was merely going to puke it back up during my next session with Nerio. So, when Pavati lowered the tray, I waved it away.

"You should eat something," she said.

I looked up at her, pointing weakly at yesterday's dinner floating beside me. "What for?"

"At least drink the water," she insisted.

I didn't bother answering. I had been marinating in acidic water for days, and Pavati expected me to trust what they poured into that cup?

She returned the next day and left after a few minutes when she realized swinging the tray in front of me wouldn't be enough to make me break.

When Nerio arrived for our session later that day, I realized just how dangerous denying their food could be. He asked his questions, I refused to answer them, and then he showered me with acid, dousing every part of me that had only just dried from the previous session.

Only this time, I had nothing left in my stomach to throw out, and so, I began to dry heave. My eyes and mouth watered as I strained to expel something, anything, from my system, but only a bit of stomach acid came up. Because surely there wasn't enough of that going around.

The heaving tired me more than if I would've puked. I slumped back against the ice wall, struggling to find the strength to stay upright even though the acid had now reached my waist. The lack of food and water fogged my mind, but I found it slightly lessened the pain from the acid, which came as a surprise *and* a relief. I couldn't focus entirely on any one train of thought, but one that seemed to stick was the reality that I would die here.

I had known something was off about me for years. I had seen the earth do strange things every now and then while growing up, though my parents never acknowledged it—I reckon for a good reason, now.

But why were these people so pressed to find my father when all he did was keep me away? Whatever the motive, I could only assume their intentions for him were less than honorable, so I could never break.

But I also couldn't survive this much longer, and I didn't want to die here. I wanted to *live*.

I spent so much of my life in the bubble created by my parents that I never truly experienced what it would be like to be normal. I wasn't allowed to visit a friend's house or get a car or even a job—though money was tight. My parents went as far as limiting my interactions with Eren and Grant, too. We were taught to restrain from physical contact, so playing tag or simply hugging each other was out of the question—at least until I was much older. I chalked it off as a bizarre parenting style they chose to uphold, but evidently, it transcended well beyond that.

While I pictured what could have been, Pavati appeared with my meal. She began, as usual, slowly balancing the tray so its contents wouldn't tumble into the filthy water. Then, an idea managed to wiggle its way out of the haze in my mind. Eureka!

I would pull Pavati down with the tray and use her as leverage so they'd free me. I just had to be sure she didn't fall on top of me.

She looked relieved when I reached for the bread. That was going to change.

After a bite, I pretended to have had enough and started to lower the bread onto the tray, watching her all the while, but instead of dropping it, I mustered all the strength I had left and slammed my arm over the tray.

But, she didn't stumble into the well as I had intended. Instead, the hand that held the rope turned clear, and straight through it went, the tray crashing over my head and into the acid.

I gaped at Pavati, speechless. I could only slightly see the silhouette of her fingers and hand now.

She sighed. "I wondered when you would try that."

My mouth still hung wide open, and before I could respond, the clearness spread from her hands, up her arms, and to her torso. Her entire body transformed into a violently moving substance before rolling out of sight.

Pavati had transformed herself into water.

SHE DIDN'T COME BACK THE NEXT DAY, AND NEITHER DID Nerio. I hadn't had food or water in over forty-eight hours. The hunger pains came with such a force that they made me double over, and I could barely keep my body above the surface. My days were numbered.

As I struggled to keep myself upright, contemplating my imminent departure from the world, I heard crunching sounds in the snow and braced myself. Pavati must've told the others of my miserable escape attempt, and now they came to teach me a lesson.

I pressed my back tightly against the ice, expecting to see Nerio sneering down at me, but instead, I saw a pale woman's face with stark black hair hanging down around it. I couldn't get a good look at her in the darkness, but I did catch her covering her nose after catching a whiff of the stench. She dropped a long rope down into the well.

I regarded it with suspicion.

"Wrap it around your waist. Hurry. We're running out of time," the woman said.

I took only a moment to weigh my odds. This could very well be a trap leading to unknown horrors elsewhere, but I would die with the known horrors here if I stayed. So, I looped the rope around my waist and tied a knot to keep it in place before tugging on it to let the woman know I was ready.

She whispered something behind her, and the rope began to haul my body upwards. The pain from my weight on the thin rope didn't matter. They gradually lifted me out of the acid that had been my home for so long, and the relief my skin felt as I became free of it was overwhelming and oh so worth it.

I took the woman's outstretched hand automatically as I marveled at being out of the acid. But, when I came face to face with her, my heart stopped.

Her eyes were pitch-black—no iris, no white, just *blackness*.

I let out a shriek as I fought to pry her hand off mine.

She held on for only a second before letting go, clutching at her throat. She gasped, her cheeks caving in, almost as though all the air had been sucked out of her. Then, she slouched over, her head rolling to the side until it hung over the edge of the hole, her black eyes wide and unmoving.

I recoiled away from her.

A man cursed under his breath, and the rope gave way hard before stabilizing. I considered untying myself, but the thought of falling into the acid from this height kept me holding onto the rope for dear life.

Finally, at the well's edge, I scrambled onto the ground only to notice two men with dark hair and the same pitch-black eyes staring back at me. Just as I readied myself to scream, the bigger man placed his finger over his mouth to silence me and took a step back himself, as though he were afraid to get too close.

"What do you want from me?" I asked as my heart thumped loudly in my chest.

Their black eyes regarded me cautiously. The smaller of the two men looked angry as he took in the woman's body on my left.

Could they be demons? I never thought I'd regret not going to church.

The larger man raised his palms to me, and I flinched. An action that usually signaled a person came in peace meant the complete opposite with Nerio.

"We're not here to hurt you," he said. "We're here to help. Can you walk?"

I attempted to get on my feet, but days without any food or water left me weak. "I'm not sure," I said.

"Well, you're gonna have to." He ran his hand through his hair, lost in thought, before turning to the smaller man. "Alright, Fintan. Get the rope and guide her back. I'll carry Candice's body. We can't leave any evidence behind."

Fintan turned to him in shock. "There is no way I'm turning my back to this thing. You do it."

"Fine. Then you can carry Candice."

"Aiden . . . You can't be serious," Fintan said, shaking his head in disgust. "Give it up. She's already dead."

"Don't you think it would be a little telling if the Icis came back to find their prisoner missing and a dead Ignis in her place? We'd face literal hell when we got back."

Fintan considered his options. "*Fuck.* Okay. But you get Candice."

Aiden walked over to the woman and awkwardly slugged her over his shoulder while Fintan pulled on the rope wrapped around me. When I didn't move, he twirled his finger, hinting for me to detangle myself, looking annoyed. Once I did, he rolled it up and draped it over his shoulder.

"Follow me, but not too closely. If you even think about touching me, you're dead," Fintan warned.

I nodded. I tugged on my rigid dress as we crouched around ice walls in what felt like a maze before reaching a clearing.

I turned to catch a glimpse of where I had been kept all this time, and my jaw nearly hit the floor. A stunning and expertly built palace made of glass loomed behind me. Or was it ice? I had never seen anything like it.

Aiden, who trailed behind us with the dead weight of Candice's body, waved for me to keep moving. "Come on. We've got to take you to Nur."

"Who's that?" I asked.

"The man you owe your life to."

Chapter Five

Nature of the Beast

We plodded through the vastness of the snowy desert for hours before reaching an inconspicuous rocky entrance to a cave. It had only taken hours because I had to stop on several occasions to catch my breath.

After what happened to their friend, Aiden and Fintan refused to come anywhere near me, let alone help. I didn't have the energy to explain that whatever happened to Candice couldn't possibly have been caused by me but found that it would be best, for now, if they believed it had. At least, then they'd keep their distance. I wasn't sure whether I could trust them yet, but it beat staying in that hell hole.

At last, the cave's labyrinth-like passages lead to a darkened, high-ceilinged room where a slim man sat on a bare wooden bench. Though the lighting from the two burning torches adorned over the bench cast a shadow over his face, I could see his eyes were pitch black, like the two that guided me here, though it didn't look quite as harsh against his deep warm-toned skin.

I realized then that the similarities in appearance may not have been by chance or choice but possibly genetic. But, what sort of gene pool supplies the blue hair of my captors and the solid black eyes of my liberators?

Though they appeared far more menacing than the others, I only hoped these people had better intentions. If they were even people at all.

The man, who looked to be in his thirties, stood as soon as we came into view, analyzing the state we were in. When he noticed the limp woman hanging over Aiden's shoulders, he grimaced.

"She did this?" he asked, motioning to me after a long pause.

Both Aiden and Fintan nodded.

He sighed. "Begin preparations for Candice and then head to the infirmary. I need both of you to keep Seraphina away from there at all costs."

They nodded again before disappearing through another passage, deeper into the cave, leaving me alone with the man.

He eyed me curiously for a moment before speaking. "I know how this may seem to you, but we mean you no harm. We have someone that has been in your exact situation, and I believe he can help you, but I won't force you to stay. You could leave if you'd like, or we could help you find an explanation for . . . all of this," he said, motioning towards my condition.

I weighed my options for a mere two seconds before agreeing to stay. After everything I had been put through and everything I had seen, I couldn't possibly leave without some answers. And I couldn't be sure it wouldn't follow me, anyway.

"Good. I'd like you to meet him, but first things first.

We need to get you to the infirmary. You're in pretty bad shape. That head wound needs to be cleaned and shut."

I let out a sigh of relief. "Please." The head wound had begun to feel numb, but I didn't particularly consider that a good thing.

"What's your name?"

"Valerie."

"Valerie, I'm Nur," he said. "I hope you understand I can't carry you after what happened to Candice. So please, follow me."

Nur wasn't much of a tour guide. He didn't utter a single word as we walked, only stealing glances back my way to be sure I kept up, but he walked slowly, and I respected him for it. Fintan had walked briskly before— almost certainly to compel me to exert myself.

The cave's walls were lined with lit torches, which kept it surprisingly toasty. It also allowed me to take in the countless chalk drawings on them. Most depicted animals, stick figures, and fire—*lots* of fire—and they appeared to have been made by children. Though, I also noticed more advanced drawings of symbols and portraits in between, which were undoubtedly created by someone who'd outgrown a sippy cup. I wondered idly how many people lived in these caves as we passed countless passages that stemmed from the hall, meaning plenty of space for people to dwell in.

Finally, Nur switched off into a room with cots and medical instruments organized over metal rolling trays and motioned for me to sit. It wasn't the most comfortable thing in the world, but after having only an ice wall to lean against for days on end, I found it heavenly. I slumped down onto the cot, giving my body the break it deserved.

After all the exertion, my legs were hot, but I still covered myself with the white blanket for a sense of security, fully aware that I would stain it with my filth. I longed to feel some warmth and pressure on my skin, and I trembled one last time as my body adjusted to the new temperature. Though my mind teemed with questions that needed answering, my eyelids weighed a ton, and I didn't have the energy to hold them up for much longer.

"I can imagine you'd like to sleep for a bit before we speak again. So I'll leave you to it," Nur said, smiling gently before turning to leave.

I drifted into a profound sleep almost instantly.

I WOKE TO THE SOUND OF WHISPERING VOICES. I HAD TO fight to open my eyes through the crustiness, but when I managed to open them, I saw Aiden, Fintan, Nur, and another man. I scrambled upright at the sight of him leaning against the wall. He had the same black hair as the others, but instead of lightless black eyes, he had the brightest blue eyes I had ever seen. He was normal —like me!

The whispering ended as soon as I moved. The man watched me, his arms crossed over his chest and his expression guarded. Aiden and Fintan stood behind him.

Nur walked in my direction but stopped before getting too close. "I'm sorry we woke you. How are you feeling?" he asked.

I thought about it for a moment. "Hungry." And, almost on cue, my stomach growled. I wrapped myself in the sheets—painfully aware of how grubby I must've looked and smelled. "How long have I been asleep?" I asked, my hoarse voice barely above a whisper.

"About fourteen hours. We figured you could use the

rest," Nur said. He turned to the men behind him and ordered Fintan to fetch food and a person named Ren.

Fintan shot a disdainful glance my way but did as he was told.

"Ren will tend to your wounds," Nur explained, and then his expression turned serious. "Valerie, I need to ask you. Have you been released?"

"Uh . . . he helped me escape," I said, nodding towards Aiden. I repositioned myself to sit up and placed my hands under my thighs to control my nerves. I glanced behind Nur at the two men who remained watching me by the entrance, attempting to find some sort of context clue that could help me decode what in the world he meant, but they only stared impassively back. What if they felt I knew more and decided to interrogate me like the others had? I couldn't go through that again. I wouldn't.

"I doubt it," Aiden said. "Calder doesn't have the means to hold her if she's been released."

Doesn't have the means to hold me? I mulled that over in my head.

"You have no idea what we're talking about, do you?" Nur asked.

I shook my head. "I'm sorry."

"It's alright," he said with a sad smile before directing his attention to the blue-eyed man. "Levi, what do you think?"

Levi pushed himself off the wall and crouched in front of me until we were at eye level. He stood close, almost too close, as he sized me up. We studied each other for a long time, only for Levi to raise his hand and cup my throat.

His grip grew tighter and tighter, and I could barely let out a scream before it occurred to me that I was being strangled. I clutched his wrist with both hands, trying to

45

pry him off me, but I hadn't eaten in days. I was beyond weak.

I mustered what little strength I had to power a swift kick to his groin, but he evaded it with ease and simply stood, pulling me up with him, forcing me to use my legs to balance myself on the cot. Otherwise, the weight of my body would've tightened his grip even further.

I could hear the two men behind him yelling, insisting that he stop, but neither thought to intervene.

Why the hell weren't they stopping him?

As abruptly as he started, he dropped me, and my knees hit the cot hard. I took in massive pulls of air, massaging my neck where his hand used to be, as the blood rushed back to my head.

People gathered around the entrance at the sound of the commotion—all dark-haired and black-eyed.

They're no better than the others! I need to get the fuck out of here.

"Damnit, Levi! What do you think you're doing?" Nur shouted, running over to me. But, still, not close enough to risk contact. He grabbed a packet of ice from a small fridge in the corner of the room, placed it on a tray, and pushed it towards me. I set it over the right side of my neck that ached the most.

"I needed to test whether she was capable of draining me like she did Candice. Looks like she can't," he said, as cool as a cucumber. As if he hadn't just strangled me.

I had never wanted to punch someone in the face quite as much as I did right then.

"You could've done that without traumatizing her," Nur said.

"If she isn't aware of how she does it, I had to convince her body she needed to. Also, I'd suggest learning her intentions before honoring her as your guest," he said.

Then, he turned towards the crowd, who watched in disbelief and laughed. "What a drastic change of heart you all have had since my day."

"Are you okay?" Nur asked, examining me from afar.

I nodded but didn't look at him. Instead, I watched Levi, readying myself to run if he took another step in my direction.

But, Levi moseyed back towards his perch against the wall. "I couldn't drain her, and she couldn't drain me. We needed to know, and now we know."

I was so caught up with the unexpected strangulation, I hadn't noticed the crowd had attracted unwanted attention. A woman yelled in the halls for people to move out of her way.

Nur became alert and looked to Aiden, who still stood in shock at what he'd just seen. "Is that Seraphina? Don't let her in here."

Just as Aiden began to peer over the others to check, a tiny woman with black hair cut close to her scalp parted the crowd. Aiden seized her arm to veer her back, but her arm became engulfed in flames, and he recoiled.

She charged towards me, as far as her short legs could take her. Her face twisted in rage.

I jumped off the cot and back-peddled, aiming to keep the distance between us. Nur wanted Seraphina to stay away, and now I understood why.

She crossed the threshold, but as soon as she came into Levi's view, he raised his arm directly in front of her, and a barrier of bright blue flames shot from them, roaring between us.

She changed course and barged towards him instead. "Let me through," she snarled.

Levi cocked his head to the side in mock bewilderment. The difference in their height would have been comical if it weren't for the fact that she actively sought to kill me, and the only person running to my defense now strangled me only minutes ago. "Now, why would I do that?"

"I'm not joking, Levi. Clear it," she demanded.

"Neither am I," he said. "Candice brought this onto herself. You don't make physical contact with an unknown elemental. We all know this."

Seraphina glared at him. When she realized he wasn't going to budge, she took one last fiery glance my way before storming out, violently pushing her way through the crowd that seemed fascinated by the upheaval.

The room boiled with the heat from the blue flames. When Levi decided she was far enough away, he motioned towards them, and they disappeared. Just like that. Levi was anything *but* ordinary.

This has got to be a fever dream—a vivid one. This isn't possible.

My damp skin dripped with sweat, and my head swarmed with dizziness. Considering my beyond-dehydrated state, I couldn't afford to lose a single drop of fluid.

Nur watched me settle into the cot furthest from the entrance. He seemed to say something to the crowd before they began to disperse, but I couldn't hear a thing. I laid my head on the pillow to ground myself, eyeing Levi warily, who watched me too, before ultimately passing out.

Chapter Six

Stone the Crows

I woke up in a panic. I was beginning to get pretty sick of passing out and the disorientation that followed. I looked around to be sure I was alone before propping myself upright and stretching my stiff limbs. Amazingly, I felt okay. Good, even. Sure, I was still ravenously hungry, but I didn't feel weak, cold, or thirsty anymore. I also noticed I was no longer in my funeral getup but in a basic brown smock.

I frowned. The idea of someone undressing me while I slept made me uneasy, and I wrapped the sheets around myself, anxiously hoping it wasn't one of the men.

I heard a sound near the entrance, and when I saw the figure standing there, my heart nearly burst out of my chest. It beat so fast that I feared it would break through my ribcage and collapse at my feet. "*Eren?*" I breathed. "Oh my god, I'm dead! I died!"

He rushed towards me, wrapping me in his arms to soothe me. I clung to him, taking in the feel of him in my arms and his air-dried, earthy smell—everything to assure me that this was actually happening. I wanted to shout for joy, but there was something that wasn't right about this.

If I died and got to see my brother, then surely this meant that I was in heaven. But, if I died in the lake, everything would have irrefutably been hell after that point. And my brother didn't belong in hell. I pulled him off me, examining him, searching for any sign of abuse.

"Val. Val, stop," he protested.

I did, but only because it astounded me to hear his voice after so long. After I made peace with the fact that I would never hear it again. "Did they hurt you?"

"No, but they hurt you," he said, spotting the bruise around my neck and the gash on my head.

"You look okay. Are you okay?"

"I am. I promise. Please, calm down. I have to talk to you before they get back," Eren said, swatting my hand away from his hair. "We're not dead, Val!"

"But you're here . . ."

"I know, but I need you to listen," Eren insisted, holding my arms down at my sides. "These people, they're not human. They can do things, and, well, we can too. We have...abilities. An ethos, they call it. Dad and Grant do, too. Even Mom! She hid us from this place, but this is where we're from—where we belong. I know this sounds crazy—"

"I understand," I said, but I was only half-listening, completely in awe of hearing Eren speak to me. Yet, even with my shock, I could accept everything he told me. My mind had hinted as much a long time ago. "But we mourned you, Eren. We *grieved*. Couldn't you have at least found a way to let us know you were okay?"

"Don't you think I would've if I knew how? Look around, Val. This isn't Alaska. I'm not even sure this is the same dimension. But I came running the moment I heard the others talking about you."

I drew him into my arms and hugged him with all my might, marveling at the miracle of this moment, when a woman with blue-tinged hair rounded the corner into the room behind him, and a bolt of dread hit me.

They came for me—I knew they would. My fight-or-flight reflex kicked in, but fleeing wasn't an option while the woman blocked our exit, so I immediately jumped off my cot to stand between her and Eren, priming myself to fight.

The woman paused when she saw my reaction, but Eren placed his hand on my shoulder and pulled me back.

"Don't freak out," he said. "That's just Ren. She healed you."

"I don't know what my people did to you in Reota," Ren said, "but I'm not like them. I won't hurt you. I bring sustenance," she said, raising a tray that appeared to be carrying food. She took small steps in my direction, but I couldn't help myself from tensing up. She looked identical to Calder and the blue-haired brothers—identical to Nerio.

Eren tugged on my arm until I finally gave in and sunk into the cot beside him. This woman wasn't charging at me or threatening to hurt me—yet, anyway. And it looked as if Eren knew her, and he wouldn't let anyone harm me. So I tried my best to relax, but even so, my eyes followed her every move.

"How are you feeling?" she asked, still keeping her distance from me.

"Surprisingly . . . better." I couldn't grasp how since there weren't any IVs attached to me, and I couldn't see any lying around. "How did you do it?"

"It's what I do," she answered with a smile.

"She can infuse bodies with magical healing water," Eren explained, completely fascinated.

She laughed. "It's not magical, just the purest form of it. The rest comes naturally."

I looked down at my smock questioningly.

"I cleaned you up while you slept, too. It was the safest way. I hope you don't mind," Ren said.

"Thank you." I didn't like the idea of anyone doing anything to me as I slept, but at least it had been another woman. Of course, they were also under the impression that I couldn't be touched, so I couldn't really blame her.

She placed the tray on the cot next to me. "I'll leave you two, so you can catch up, but please eat and have some water. You were dehydrated and are still malnourished. That's not a good combination."

I nodded. Eren grabbed the tray and placed it on my lap. It was a considerably large loaf of bread paired with chicken and cheese, and I happily dug in. I eyed the water in the cup, trying to make out the color, but it was too dark in here to tell. Safer not to risk it. I pushed it away.

As I ate, Eren went on to illuminate me on what he had learned. He told me our father had taken him to the lake where he had been dragged in by some unknown entity—like I had. I paused and held his hand as he retold the pain of the acidic lake and how he also drowned and appeared here, but it astounded me that the blue-haired monsters didn't torture him for information as they did me. As glad as I was to hear that, it mystified me all the same.

Eren went on to tell me that he fled from the Icis and found this cave, where the Ignis took him in, only to be told he wasn't human at all but a being that could harness the power of an element—an elemental.

The Ventus controlled the air and could be identified

by their white hair and green eyes—like Eren, Grant, and our mother.

The Natura, who mastered the earth, had brown hair and eyes—like our father.

The Ignis, born with black hair and matching black eyes, could summon and manipulate fire at will.

And lastly, my captors, the Icis, whose genetics gave them the odd blue-colored hair and eyes, had the power to control water.

I wondered how long it took him to accept such an extraordinary concept. Seeing as he surrounded himself with outlandish worlds in his free time, it probably wasn't too difficult for him. I would just have to take his word for it. At this point, considering everything I had seen and experienced, it didn't seem too far-fetched.

"Where would that leave me?" I asked since my brown hair and green eyes didn't fit into any of the molds he described.

"That's the thing. So you're both Natura *and* Ventus. Which turns out is, like, basically unheard of, which is why I think the Icis did what they did," he said, looking down at his hands.

He asked for specifics about my time with them and, though I didn't wish to relive it, I also didn't want to lie, so I told him—leaving only the darker bits out. Of course, he didn't need to hear that.

"I want to kill every last one of them for what they did to you," he said after a long pause. His hands clenched into fists.

"You and me both," I muttered. "But it's over now."

We sat quietly while I processed the information, but a question continued to gnaw at me. "Why would Dad take us to the lake, Eren?" I asked. "Why would he cast us into this world, knowing how they'd respond?"

"Maybe we were seen by a Ventus or a Natura, and he panicked. Mom and Dad weren't supposed to be together, let alone have us. But, they did, so now here we are," he said, shrugging. "Perhaps he felt what lay in store for us here couldn't be worse than what awaited us there."

I mulled that over, recalling when Calder referred to me as an impurity and how he guessed that our father hid us, but something was off. "I don't understand. Why didn't you or Grant turn out like me? I mean, we have the same parents. And Grant and I are twins."

"I don't know. The only other person like you is a guy named Levi, but he's an only child. I'm guessing because you were their firstborn?"

I shrugged. My head had begun to ache, attempting to make sense of it all. "And yeah," I said. "I met Levi."

He picked up on my tone. "I hear he's not the friendliest guy."

"That's the understatement of the year."

Eren continued despite my comment. "He's half Ignis, half Icis which is why he has their black hair, but the Icis' blue eyes. They say he killed a ton of people when he got his powers. Not on purpose, but still," he added, raising his brows. He spoke almost as though he admired him.

"Grant and Warren," I said, my voice barely above a whisper, "they think you're dead, Eren."

"I know."

"I wish there was some way we could tell them you're alive."

Eren placed his hands on mine. "We'll see them again, Val. But we can't leave just yet."

"Why not?"

"Don't you think it's weird, now that we're finding out about all this, that our mother, who had magical powers, died in a *car accident*?"

"I guess so."

"I think they killed Mom, Val," he said. "I think they found out about you and, when she wouldn't give you up, I think they killed her."

"Who's they?"

"That's what I'd like to find out."

LATER THAT DAY, AN IGNIS NAMED CORA ANNOUNCED herself to us while a piece of bread hung from her mouth. Levi came in behind her—much to Eren's excitement and my disdain. Eren's hand fumbled to draw my attention to Levi as if someone could possibly overlook him. Then, Cora announced Ren had sent her to cauterize my head wound.

I didn't like the sound of that. Not one bit.

She swallowed her mouthful and tied her sleek black hair into a ponytail. "Look, I've got things to do," she said. "So you either let me do my thing now, or I'll get Ren in here to argue with you until you eventually fold, and *then* I do my thing. The end result is the same. It's happening."

I looked to Eren, who nodded in her direction for me to let her. "Fine, I guess."

Cora made her way over but stopped shortly before reaching me. "And don't go leaching the air out of me, either. It'll hurt, but it's gotta be done. Levi's here to hold you still for me since he's immune to you. Just know that if you kill me, I'll haunt you forever."

"I don't really know how I do it, but okay."

"Awesome," she said. "That makes me feel a whole lot better. Thank you."

I stretched out onto the cot while Levi made his way to me until he hovered over my head, and I glared at him.

"Still haven't forgiven me?" he asked with a sly smile.

"How could I? Forgiveness follows an apology, and I have yet to receive one."

He shot me a dazzling grin, but instead of apologizing like I thought he would, he ordered in a deep, authoritative tone that I place my hands behind my back, catching me off guard. My ears burned, and I looked away, unable to meet his eyes, before doing as I was told.

Levi placed his warm and surprisingly soft hands on either side of my head to keep me still. I closed my eyes to keep my face from giving me away—forever grateful his gift involved fire and not reading minds—and took a deep breath, concentrating on the opposite of killing someone.

Puppies. I imagined a howl of Siberian husky pups frolicking in a grassy field.

Cora placed her hot fingertips on my forehead.

Puppies, back to puppies. They're climbing on top of me now, tails wagging, yapping happily.

Surging heat.

The puppies nudge their tiny little heads into me, giving me kisses.

"Son of a . . . *bitch*," I cursed as the sizzle snapped me back to reality, and the pain began to register. Levi's hands tightened as I tried to steer away.

Puppies, puppies, puppies . . .

Then, he let go. I opened my eyes and patted the wound to lessen the throbbing pain, but the sliver continued to pulsate. Then, Levi placed something in my hand. Pills.

"It's for the pain," he said.

Eren shot out of his cot. "Let me get you some water to wash them down with."

I instantly popped the two mammoth-sized pills into

my mouth and swallowed them, suppressing my instinct to gag. "I'm good, Eren. Thanks, though!"

Levi eyed me curiously but took his leave after announcing his job here was done.

"Okay, then," Eren mumbled, placing the cup back in its place. "I have a few things I need to do, but I'll be back. Will you be alright?"

"She'll be fine," Cora assured him. "I'll keep her company."

Just as he disappeared out of view, Ren rounded the corner with a lanky black-haired, black-eyed boy, who looked to be no older than twenty, leaning against her shoulder for support as he bled out of his nose.

"What now, Zoran?" Cora whined, running to help Ren get him into a cot.

But Ren answered instead. "He thought it wise to pick a fight with Fintan again."

"Someone's gotta knock him down a few pegs," Zoran said, wiping his bloody nose with the back of his hand. "The guy's a total jerk."

Cora laughed. "Yeah? Well, it looks like you got knocked down. Not Fintan," she said before turning to me. "He's a regular."

"I am not!" he protested.

"He really is," Ren said, making both Zoran and Cora laugh, and she examined me while she placed an ice pack on Zoran's nose. "How are you feeling?"

I smiled. "Good, thank you."

"Great. I washed you as best I could here, but I wasn't able to do much. Especially to your hair. But Cora can show you to our bathing room so you can freshen up."

"Oh, that won't be necessary. I'm okay."

Cora walked over to a storage bin, where she pulled out

folded clothes and a towel before turning to me. "It is *absolutely* necessary. You look rough."

"Gee, thanks," I muttered. I hopped off the cot and motioned for Cora to lead the way, peeved they refused to accept my polite decline to their offer. Immersing myself in water was the absolute last thing in the world I wanted to do, but she walked ahead, oblivious to my mood. Quite happily, actually. While the skip in her step made her ponytail bounce sweetly behind her, it left me wrangling against the urge to trip her.

She led me through a whirlwind of pathways. I didn't bother trying to remember the route. I didn't plan to visit that particular room very often, but the kitchen's, on the other hand, I needed to learn.

I peered into the rooms as we passed them. Many looked empty, with a few housing crates and large boxes. Then, we passed a room laden with toys, and as I peered in further, I noticed children huddled together playing Pat-a-Cake.

I smiled, thinking how cute they were until one of them glanced in my direction. The little boy's black eyes stared back at me, and I looked away, rushing to catch up to Cora. Somehow, I hadn't fully grasped that these people would have appeared that way since birth. It gave me the creeps, and I rubbed my arms to rid them of the goosebumps.

The other rooms were filled with adults talking casually amongst themselves. They'd stop and look up when they heard us passing by, their eyes narrowing in suspicion, because to them, *I* was the freak—the unnatural creation of two lawbreakers on the run. So, right now, they trusted me about as much as I trusted them.

Finally, Cora stopped in front of an opening in the rock

wall, and I could hear flowing water coming from within it. I took a tiny, silent breath to steady myself.

Cora pounded her fist against the rock, and the sound reverberated into the room. "I've got an impurity that needs to bathe! So, finish whatever you're doing now, 'cause I'm about to set her loose in here!"

A commotion ensued. Voices were hushed, things were dropped, and people were running before we saw a young couple emerge wrapped in towels, clutching their clothes to their chests as they sidestepped us. They didn't look up, but I saw the girl's cheeks burning a bright red.

Cora giggled.

"You really know how to clear a room, huh?" I asked.

"All I had to do was mention you," she said, winking at me. "Take these." Cora handed me the clothes and a towel, careful not to touch me. "Everything else you need is in there. Have fun!" She waved goodbye to me, obnoxiously, I might add, as I made my way into the room.

The only light source in the dim cave room came from torches placed in even intervals on the walls. I guess you didn't need to bother with electricity when you could muster fire at the drop of a hat.

I followed the sound of the rushing water until I saw an underground river that traversed the room. It flowed gently enough that I didn't think there would be any danger stepping into it, but I had no intention of doing so. Instead, I made my way to a station that offered soap and other toiletries alongside a medium-sized mirror placed against the wall. I avoided the mirror but grabbed a bar of soap, and, oddly enough, it was lettered, *Dove.*

How in the world do they have access to Dove soap?

I grabbed it anyway, along with a generic brand toothpaste and deodorant. I skipped the shampoo and conditioner, which would require me to dip my head into the water—a big no-no.

I trudged along the edge of the river before ultimately picking a spot and sat by its edge. There was no getting out of this. I had to come out at least a bit changed, but my heart raced at the thought of the water touching my skin. What if this was all a ploy to hurt me again? I had no way to know since, in the dimness of the room, the river's water looked no different than the acid I had been forced to live in.

I closed my eyes, trying to quiet my thoughts. I removed my smock and dipped it into the water to use as a shower rag, hoping to avoid getting into the river altogether. I could feel the water run down my fingertips and took a huge breath as my pulse quickened. The water ran cold, and I could swear I felt it sting through the bitter chill, which caused me to instantly break into tears. I pressed my face into my arm to stifle the sobs and bit down to distract myself from a pain that I surely imagined to focus on one that was real. I didn't know if Cora planned to go off somewhere to give me privacy or if she was waiting for me by the entrance, but I didn't want her to hear me.

The crying made my nose run and puddle over my upper lip until it spilled over and onto my chin. Somehow, I had managed to get filthier than before. I figured my tears, and now my mucus, desensitized my face to the water, so I dragged the smock over my face after having lathered it with soap.

Bad idea. Stupid.

I sniffed and, just when I thought things couldn't get any worse, soapy water rushed into my nostrils, stinging my nasal passages and throat, making me cry all the more. At this point, I was bathing in self-pity.

I kept my mouth and eyes shut between my sobs and blindly dragged the soap around my body, focusing on my underarms and private areas—the leading cause of the complaints. I combed my hair out with my fingers, massaged soap into the crusty areas, and wiped it off with the smock until it was somewhat cleaner.

After what felt like a brutal eternity, I decided enough was enough and got dressed in the fresh clothing Cora provided for me: a tattered brown shirt and loose-fitted jeans, paired with basic worn sneakers.

I stepped out and, from the look on Cora's face, I wasn't as successful at masking my hysteria as I thought I'd been.

"It echoes," she said, motioning around the walls of the cave. She didn't say anything else, bless her heart, but took my dirty smock and flung it into a bin near the opening.

She announced she'd be taking me to the common area of their compound so that I could eat, which I was more than happy about—anything to take my mind off my traumatic bathing experience. I trailed behind her until we came across an opening with a painting over it, and I laughed as I took in the bizarre depiction of a chicken in the style of Elvis Presley. The idea seemed like something a child would think up, but the work itself was one of a skillful artist.

Cora followed my gaze. "Oh, that's Seraphina's creation. She takes requests from the kids. I heard you two met," she said, a knowing smile playing on her lips.

"You could say that, though I don't think Seraphina likes me very much."

"Don't take it personally. Seraphina doesn't like anyone," she said, only to place her finger to her lips as she considered it. "Well, other than her best friend Candice— whom you killed. So, maybe it is personal."

"I didn't mean to! I didn't even know I could—"

"I know," she reassured me. "I'm sure she does too, but I wouldn't expect much from her in the form of friendship any time soon. That one can really hold a grudge."

I couldn't believe my first interaction with these people turned out to be fatal, leaving me to forever watch my back from a woman who not only embodied fire with her intensity but quite literally *was* the fire.

When did my luck run out?

Maybe two months ago, when I bought a Snickers bar from the vending machine outside Mr. Lindat's bookstore, and two came out.

Worth it.

As we entered the common area, everybody's head snapped in our direction. Most snatched their belongings and left through a second exit on the furthermost wall, wanting absolutely nothing to do with me. The remaining Ignis, who refused to be driven out, gravitated towards the rows of benches that faced a television and whispered amongst themselves, forming a tangible tension in the room.

I followed Cora to their dining area, trying not to let them get to me, only to get distracted when I saw three fridges lined up against the wall.

"Are those . . . connected?" I asked, unable to comprehend how they could have wired the cave with electricity.

"No, they're decorative."

Though she had to be kidding, her expression remained serious.

She laughed. "Of course, they're connected! The Icis have windmills above ground, but we managed to sneak some down here. Took a lot of work, though, so we settled with only having any in this room and the infirmary. We didn't want to test our luck. Anyway, we're happy so long as our food stays fresh and our television's plugged in," she explained. When she caught me eyeing the TV, she added that they survived off their extensive DVD collection. She walked over to one of the fridges, procuring two packaged meals.

"That wasn't made for her!" a woman, who sat across the room, called out.

"I don't care!" Cora answered. "If you have a problem with it, take it up with Nur."

The woman muttered something angrily to the others, but Cora ignored her.

She motioned to sit with her at one of the tables before handing me one of the bundles.

"Everyone's treating me like I'm a leper. Why aren't you?" I asked as I built a sandwich with the bread, cheese, and chicken I pulled out.

Don't get me wrong, I cherished having someone to talk to, but I didn't understand why Cora didn't condemn me like the rest of them did. It was one of her kind that I killed after all, even if I did so unintentionally. She had just as much reason to hate me as the rest of them.

She thought about it for a moment, fiddling with a plain silver bracelet on her wrist. "To be perfectly honest with you, I need a powerful friend."

I laughed, nearly choking on a wedge of cheese. "How do you get that from this?" I asked once I recovered, pointing at my face. "I hate to break it to you, Cora, but I'm far from powerful. I'm afraid you've been duped."

"Do you see Aiden over there?" she asked, and I followed her gaze to see him talking with the group huddled in the corner. He must've just walked in.

I nodded.

"Well, he's supposed to be our authority, not Nur. For as long as we've existed, no ethos could rival the element to

63

steel manipulation, so whoever it cycled to would automatically be appointed the authority."

"What makes that power so strong?"

"Think about it. It creates a nearly indestructible solid out of gases, liquids, and even thin air. Killing is a breeze if you have unlimited access to metal. Still, though, your ability to drain the air out of people at will is way cooler."

I scoffed. "Not when everyone's afraid to touch you."

"I don't think they grasp that you could turn it on and off. I'm sure the rest will get over it once they understand how it works," Cora said. "But as formidable as the element to steel manipulation is, when Levi's mother evoked him, it changed everything. No one could oppose Levi to take the title, but Levi thought it beneath him and appointed Nur in his place. Everyone pretends to look down on you for being impure, but Levi is too, and he has more influence over what goes on here than Aiden and even Nur himself, though technically Nur's our authority. So, I'm doing you a favor that I hope I can cash in later," she added after a short pause.

I couldn't help but feel a little used. Obviously, Cora didn't know me very well, but I thought that maybe she understood what it was like to be an outsider in one way or another and intended to make me feel more at ease. I didn't see anyone else lining up to help me, so I couldn't be too annoyed with her. Beggars can't be choosers, after all.

I watched Aiden from across the room, trying to catch any sign of what he was capable of. I couldn't imagine what transforming fire into steel even looked like. I also couldn't help remembering how he simply backed off when the bloodthirsty Seraphina barged into the infirmary to end me. Perhaps he didn't feel the need to fight his own kind to defend me—someone he doesn't know or possibly even likes. Who knows? I might've done the same if the situation were reversed.

Aiden stood chatting with the group seated on the benches. One of them laughed at something he said, and his answering smile illuminated the room. His features were quite handsome if you could get past the two black voids centered on his face.

He must've sensed me staring since he turned to us and made his way to our table. Cora brushed off the bread crumbs resting on the corner of her mouth and straightened herself out.

"What are you two conspiring about over here?" he asked with a mischievous smirk.

"We were just nailing down the specifics for our plan to take over the world," I said, winking at Cora. For the first time since I met her, she seemed to have nothing to say.

She smiled timidly, nodding in agreement.

He chuckled. "Well, if you need any help with that, you know where to find me."

"Actually, we do. Have you seen my brother anywhere?" I longed to see him again. My mind had begun to consider that perhaps I had imagined the reunion altogether.

"I saw him walking down the corridor about an hour ago, but I haven't seen him since," he said. "I'll let him know you're looking for him if I do."

"I appreciate that."

He tipped an invisible top hat to each of us before turning back to sit with the others.

I watched Cora as she stared at his retreating back.

"What?" she asked when she caught me eyeing her.

I smiled. "Oh, nothing. I just find it odd that you've managed to be so thorough in filling me in when it comes to everything else, only to leave out that you have a thing for Aiden."

She rolled her eyes. "You're told you have powers, and you choose to focus on this?"

"It's a riveting detail," I said. "I can't believe you left it out."

"Shut up."

"Now, I can't help but wonder what else you're keeping from me. I mean, are vampires real, too?"

She chuckled. "*Stop.*"

"What about werewolves?"

She snatched my bundle from my hands and threw it into the bin by the fridge.

"Cora!" I protested, laughing all the while. "There was still a block of cheese in there."

"The horse is dead. Put the stick down," she said. "Now, follow me. Another word about Aiden, and I'll take you straight to Seraphina. Who, by the way, is Aiden's ex, so I wouldn't go joking about this to anyone else."

"If I did, I don't think I'd be Seraphina's target anymore, though, would I? It might even be in my best interest."

Cora nodded, smiling. "Touché."

I followed her out of the common room and towards our next destination in higher spirits. No matter her motive for taking me under her wing, I was grateful, and she didn't seem to be minding it much either.

As we walked down the hallway, a kid, no more than ten years old, ran into us.

Initially, I thought they might've been a girl since they seemed to have a more feminine bone structure, but they were completely hairless—no hair, no eyebrows, no lashes. I did my best not to flinch at the black eyes, hoping I'd get used to seeing them soon. The shock had to wear off at some point, right?

"Oh!" Cora exclaimed, grabbing the kid by their shoulders and facing them to me. "This is my little sister, Fiametta," she said, looking down at her. "This is Valerie, a Natura that's going to stay with us for a while. Fiametta, say hi," she nudged.

Fiametta looked up at me, smiled, and waved before prancing off.

"She's not much of a talker. Something I wish I could say about Iri, my other sister."

I waved her away. "It's no biggie. And I'm so sorry," I added.

She laughed. "What for?"

I motioned at my scalp. "Is Fiametta . . . I mean, is she okay?"

"Oh! Yeah, she's not sick or anything. Her ethos just keeps her body temperature too high for any hair to grow."

"What can she do?" I asked.

Cora's expression sobered up. "She can self-combust."

"What? That's so cool! Can you do that, too?"

She shook her head. "I can't generate fire." And though she strove to sound aloof, her tone, laced with regret, betrayed her.

I didn't say anything, not wanting to upset her further.

But Cora shook the feeling and simpered at me. "But I can break bones," she settled, doing mock karate punches in the air. "No one shares the same ethos, and some are more underwhelming than others. Take mine, for example. I have a touch ability; I can cauterize, as you well know," she said, pointing at the raised scar on my forehead. "An ethos like mine is mostly useful in kitchens and infirmaries, but you don't want to taste my cooking. While a ranged ethos like Fiametta's is reserved for combat. You can't help what you're born with," she added with a shrug. She kept her voice detached, but I could tell it was a sore topic for her.

"Working in kitchens and infirmaries is honorable work, Cora," I said. "You're just as important, if not more so, than the other guys. I mean, you're needed on a daily basis. You make life here possible, while the fighters do nothing until . . . well until they have to do something."

"You sound like my mother," Cora grumbled.

We made it back to the infirmary, where Zoran sat balancing playing cards in the form of a castle. He managed to get it pretty high, too.

"Oh, goody. You're still here," Cora muttered.

Zoran didn't look at her. "Has Fintan left to the Origin yet?"

"Nope."

"Then, here I'll remain," he said, his eyes wide with focus as he held a wobbly card still with his index finger.

"The Origin?" I asked.

"Where you come from," she said. "We have a group that travels through the lake for supplies every so often. It's how all this stuff got here."

I plopped myself onto the cot, shuddering at the thought of having to suffer through the agonizing lake time and time again. If it were up to me, the Ignis would have to settle with what little they had.

I reminded Cora to tell Eren I was looking for him when she declared she had errands to run, more than a bit hurt that he didn't feel the need to stay by me after being apart for so long. But then again, he knew I was alive, while I thought I had lost him forever.

I considered making small talk with Zoran, but he seemed consumed with his castle of cards, so I laid back and tried to force myself to sleep instead.

CHAPTER SEVEN

WOLF IN SHEEP'S CLOTHING

EREN

EVEN THOUGH THE WINTRY AIR BURNED MY LUNGS, I forced myself into a jog.

They promised me it would be a menial task for the greater good, and that's why I agreed so wholeheartedly, but no one told me my sister would be involved in this.

I reached their gates, which had already begun to open for me. Laec and Salil waited for me by the entrance, having already seen me coming.

"Back so soon?" Laec asked.

"Take me to Calder. Right now."

Salil laughed. "Now, now, little Ventus. You're in no position to be making demands."

"I just had a run-in with my sister at the Ignis compound where she told me she had been held and tortured by you. So yeah, I demand an explanation."

That did it. The brothers locked eyes with each other

and marched in what I assumed was Calder's general direction.

Livid as I was, I couldn't stop myself from soaking in the breathtaking city of Reota. It would be a crime not to admire the magnificent architecture of this ice world. It looked like one continuous block of ice, with rooms sculpted directly into it and polished art chiseled into every inch of the walls.

It was clear that while the Ignis only survived in their cave-dwelling, the Icis thrived on the surface. The halls bustled with people going about their daily tasks. And no one looked surprised to see me among them.

For the first time in my life, I didn't feel like an outsider. No one gawked at me as I walked past or cracked a joke at my expense because I *belonged* here. In the Oasis, the white pigment of my hair wasn't used as ammunition to single me out from the rest. On the contrary, I was marveled. The Icis looked to me with esteem, recognizing that I wasn't an ordinary man but a Ventus—born with a purpose they couldn't replicate. Singular. Here, I was *someone*.

I could never tire of this place.

But, when the brothers led me into Calder's office, my confidence dwindled. In Calder's presence, I did *not* belong.

He stood hunched over his desk, glossing over a set of documents, and looked up when we came in. He appeared mildly annoyed at the intrusion but listened intently at Salil's explanation for it.

"Your sister?" Calder asked me.

"Yes," I said, my expression hard. "That was my sister you tortured." I wanted to say more but held my tongue. This wasn't someone I could lose my cool around.

He walked around the table, lost in thought, before planting himself in front of me, and I inadvertently cowered. Though he harnessed the power to transform water into steel, he still dedicated considerable time and effort to bulk up, adding yet another reason to fear him in the already long list of reasons.

The lines around his eyes deepened as he narrowed them, and he cracked his fingers. "Forgive me, Eren, but I find myself unable to wrap my mind around why you never thought to mention your sister was impure."

"You told me about Levi, but she looks nothing like him," I said, piqued at the hint of suspicion in his tone. "How was I supposed to know?"

He tilted his head to the side. "So, when we detailed Levi's sacrilegious conception, the fact that your father is a Natura and your mother a Ventus didn't 'connect the dots' for you?"

I froze, cursing at myself for having allowed my anger to lead me here. Of course, my mind had gone straight to how Valerie looked nothing like Grant and me. But how do I tell Calder that I had hoped it was only because it had skipped her entirely?

He would not appreciate nor understand my wishful thinking because I loved my sister, and I couldn't see Calder loving anyone.

Calder watched me until, finally, he realized I had no clue how to justify my lapse in logic. "Well, this changes everything," he said. "They're less likely to suspect you now, which is good. But now, we have two impurities to dispose of. That will be a challenge even if your sister hasn't been evoked."

I backed away from him, shaking my head. "No. I agreed to help you when it came to Levi, but no way in hell will I help you hurt Valerie. She's not like him!"

Calder's expression morphed into what I assumed he intended to be sympathy, though it reeked of insincerity.

"She is every bit as dangerous as Levi, Eren, maybe even more so. Levi has already been evoked and has shown no signs of wanting to exert his power over us, but we don't know how she'll react if she's given the same opportunity. We can't give her that chance. If she realizes the kind of power she possesses, we're finished."

I ran my fingers through my hair, anxious to get out of here. Anxious to return to the Ignis compound, grab Valerie, and return home. I achieved nothing by coming here, but perhaps give Calder more reason to believe I was the best man for the job, even if I didn't want it anymore. Even if it meant betraying my family.

"Come," Calder said. "She's been asking to speak with you."

My face lit up. "She has?"

He smiled—another contrived look for him. "Yes. Perhaps she can shed some light on the situation."

As much as I didn't want to even consider this anymore, I couldn't pass up the chance to see her again. If anyone could understand my hesitation and help me find a way out of this, it would be her spirit.

I RETURNED TO THE IGNIS COMPOUND, EMOTIONALLY battered but resolute. This was the pivotal moment I had witnessed repeatedly on the screen where the hero had to decide whether he would side with his heart, selfish as it may be, or with what he knew to be right—no matter the personal toll. I always told myself that I, too, would be strong enough to do the right thing if made to choose.

Now, with the same circumstance presenting itself before me, I needed to come to terms with the fact that I was no longer a kid in need of protection. No longer a kid that would cry for any sort of accolade. The dilemma was no longer a hypothetical to reflect on between commercial breaks.

I wiped my tears away and stood tall. It was time to be the man I had always strived to be.

Chapter Eight

Pecking Order

VALERIE

I couldn't sleep, but that didn't stop me from spending all day trying.

At one point, I managed to calm my thoughts and felt relieved that eventually, I'd slip into unconsciousness when Zoran's house of cards went tumbling down, knocking me right back to where I started. I sighed.

"Sorry," he whispered.

"It's okay," I said, turning to face him. "I've got too much running through my head, anyway."

"I bet. It's gotta be tough having this sprung on you all at once," Zoran said, his face lighting up as he thought of something. "Has anyone gone over our history with you yet?"

I shook my head.

"Well, since you can't sleep, would you like to hear it? It makes for one hell of a bedtime story."

"Sure," I said, nestling against my pillow. "I'd like that."

He clapped his hands together in anticipation, making me giggle. "Essentially, it all started when Vulcan, the god of fire; Mokosh, the goddess of the earth; Æther, the god of the wind; and Nereus, the god of the sea mixed their . . . otherworldly blood with humans for the first time thousands of years ago. We don't know why they decided to do so or how, but we have countless theories that we can dive into later. But, it led to our creation—the elementals."

"We had a rocky start. The first generations were killed by humans almost to the brink of extinction. You see, we were outnumbered, and humans are so easily threatened by anything they don't understand."

"They called the Natura and Icis fairies or witches—depending on the region, the Ignis demons, and the Ventus angels. That's what being able to fly gets you," he scoffed. "But, in the end, the elementals realized trying to coexist with humans was damn near impossible, so they created the Oasis," he said, waving his hands around us.

"It didn't always look like this," he added when he noticed my blasé expression. "But, this world we created wasn't enough for us to fully harness our powers. Sure, they created a mock sun, wind, and sea on this side of the lake, but the real thing is on the other side. Then, a rumor spread of a Natura that took it upon himself to travel back to the Origin. Before we could be sure he was, in fact, a Natura, the humans killed him."

"He didn't get very far," I said. "So, no harm done then, right?"

"Not exactly. The elementals had collectively agreed to stay in the Oasis, so every other faction felt cheated when they heard about it. Then, the Natura figured they might as well leave to the Origin since they were being accused of breaking the pact anyway, and the Ventus followed suit, claiming they'd track and persecute them for abandoning the agreement. It all turned out to be a ruse to get the rest of us to accept it, but once they left, we could do nothing about it."

"How come?" I asked. "That doesn't seem fair at all."

"Well, the Natura could easily blend into the human world, so long as they didn't flaunt their abilities like that man was said to have done, and the Ventus lived high enough in the mountains and could fly away at the first sign of a human. The Icis, on the other hand, couldn't hide their inhuman characteristics, let alone the Ignis. Humans could never come to terms with these," Zoran added, pointing at his pitless eyes and forcing a smile.

I dropped my chin to my chest to avoid his eyes as shame swept through me, recalling the terror I had felt when I first made eye contact with Candice. It must be awful to be feared and seen as evil over something entirely out of your control, like one's eye color, and it pained me to see the way it affected them.

Zoran continued, unaware of the shift in my mood. "The Ignis and Icis lived in relative harmony here until about fifteen years ago. Then, we came to find that one of our own had given birth to a son, fathered by an Icis," he said and let out a heavy sigh. "It broke whatever fragment of trust we still harbored for each other because, since our inception, it was decided in absolute that our species should never interbreed to avoid mucking the bloodlines. They thought it was best to stay as pure as our respective gods chose us to be. Unlike the ruling that we should stay in the Oasis, this wasn't up for debate. This was sacred. So, the Icis turned on us, but we weren't even aware Leviathan existed. We only found out after his mother, Udiya, evoked him twelve years after he was born, but she had kept him hidden all those years before then."

"Wait, wait, hold on," I said, trying to suppress a laugh. "Levi is short for *Leviathan*? Like the *sea serpent* . . . ?"

He pursed his lips but nodded. "Udiya had no way to know he'd be predominantly Ignis," Zoran explained. "Levi was the first of his kind. His twelve-year-old body had so much pent-up energy inside that he literally exploded when his mother evoked him, killing just about everyone in a five-mile radius, including her. Udiya never imagined that would happen. Evoking someone had never been so violent . . . " Zoran trailed off, shifting his attention to shuffling his cards, and cleared his throat before continuing.

"It all went downhill from there. The Icis thought Levi was a ploy for us to have the upper hand against them, claiming Udiya tricked the Icis into bedding her. But, since Udiya died in the blast and the Icis was never identified, the Ignis had no means to dispute the accusation, which led to what came to be known as the Purity War."

"So, the Icis stormed the cave?"

"We lived above ground back then, but the Icis destroyed Eldur, our home, with such a relish during the war that you couldn't even find ruins of it today if you tried. Our city, the place we called home for millennia, was wiped from the face of the Origin like it never existed. But, the pain of watching Eldur fall galvanized us, and that's when Nur found Levi and convinced him to help them fight against the Icis. We did the best we could, but even so, we were outnumbered and out-planned. I'm sure I don't need to tell you who won," he added bitterly.

Their tragic history rendered me speechless, and we sat in silence together, neither of us knowing what else to say. I reached out to Zoran only to lower my hand, remembering my touch wouldn't be welcome here.

But, I viewed the Ignis in a new light. The Ignis suffered through every possible indignity, only to be forced to retreat into a cave to live like scavengers. As if I needed another excuse to despise the Icis.

I wished there was something I could do or say to alleviate their suffering, but this world was still so new to me. Perhaps if I was given a chance to release and exercise my powers, then maybe I could find a way. . .

"I wonder when I'll be evoked," I said, primarily to myself, but Zoran heard me.

"That's never going to happen," he said. "They'd never allow it after what happened with Levi."

Zoran's dismissive tone was harsh. Or maybe it was his words. Though I understood their reluctance, it still gutted me to hear that I would never be able to access my full potential. Instead, I would remain in the state before metamorphosis, an eternal caterpillar in a world full of butterflies.

Forever a damsel in distress in need of rescuing, I thought and inwardly cringed.

"It's not like we have a Natura at our disposal to evoke you," Zoran muttered.

"But I'm part Ventus, right? And Eren is a Ventus."

"Natura would be your dominant element if you work the same way Levi does. You have their hair and a Ventus touch ability."

"Oh," I said, scraping my hand over my face to conceal my disappointment. My plan to convince Eren to help release my powers had been foiled before it had even fully formed.

Then again, I wasn't so easily thwarted.

I woke up out of breath, drenched in sweat. Nerio paid my dreams a visit yet again, and I could have sworn I felt his acid scorching my skin, but as I looked around to ground myself, I was in the infirmary with my body clear of any of it.

Eren sat on the edge of my cot, patting my legs. "It's okay, Val. You're okay," he said. "It was only a dream."

Only it wasn't. It had been my reality just days ago. But, I took a deep breath to steady myself anyway. "Where have you been?" I asked. "I waited for you yesterday, but you never came."

"Unloading crates the Ignis brought back from the Origin," he said, and his face grew worried. "But, there's a problem."

My body stiffened. "Tell me."

"The Icis have Grant. Dad must've taken him to the lake, too."

"No, no, no, no," I groaned. "Are you sure? I mean, how do you know?"

"Seraphina said she passed Reota on their way back and saw they had someone else in the pit. From her description, it has to be him."

I jumped to my feet, slipping on the sneakers Ren had set aside for me. "What the *fuck* is Dad thinking? What could possibly be going on up there that he thinks we're better off here?" I asked, frantically trying to tie my shoelaces only to give up and tuck them in at the sides. I couldn't concentrate. We didn't have time.

Eren shrugged. "I don't know."

"We have to find Nur," I said and grabbed his arm, hauling him along as I stormed out of the infirmary. "They need to get him out of there."

Desperation clouded my thoughts as the image of Nerio raining acid onto Grant plagued me, so we weaved chaotically through the maze, arguing over who knew the correct route to the common room. The few Ignis we passed recoiled and ran off when they saw us before we could ask for help, but thankfully, after about ten wrong turns, we saw Seraphina's chicken rendition of Elvis and heaved a sigh of relief.

Once inside, though, we were instantly let down. The Ignis stood hunched over cases of loot the scavengers had procured, with no sign of Nur among them. However, I did catch Cora reading the backs of a stack of DVD cases and beelined towards her.

Cora waved when she saw me. "Look! They found *Clueless*! I've wanted to watch this for so long."

"Where's Nur, Cora?" I asked before she could go off on one of her tangents.

"Well, hello to you, too," she muttered. "Nur and Levi lock themselves in his office after every trip doing who knows what."

"Take me to them. Please. It's important," I added when Cora continued to flip the disks over. I yanked them out of her hands and placed them back into the crate so she'd focus.

Cora laughed and raised her hands in the air. "Alright. Jeez. Follow me."

She guided us through the passages and made a sharp left, leading us to an opening with panels of wood secured over it, acting as a door. Inside, a female voice informed someone that, whatever she held in her hand, was the only bottle left.

Cora knocked three times.

"What?" the female voice asked.

"Is Nur in there? It's an emergency," Cora said.

The door swung open. Seraphina, who now appeared to be entirely baldheaded, stood with a liter bottle of rum raised in her hand. Behind her, Nur and Levi sat slumped against a desk—more than a little inebriated. Levi passed the bottle in his hand to Nur and fumbled to his feet when he saw us.

Seraphina looked murderously annoyed. "Well, if it isn't Tweedledee and Tweedledum. What the hell is she doing here?" she asked Cora.

I moved past Seraphina until I faced Nur. Well, not exactly, since he was still on the floor, but as close to facing as I was going to get. "The Icis have our brother Grant. We need to send someone in to rescue him."

Nur propped himself up unsteadily now. "Move out of the way, Sera," he demanded, his words slurring.

She glared at me for a moment before doing so.

"I can't do that," he said, clearing his throat to mask his drunkenness.

"Why not?" I asked, my brows drawing together. "You rescued Eren. And you had them save me."

"Eren came to us," he corrected. "And yes, we did rescue you, but look where that got us. Candice is dead. The feeling that we took an unnecessary risk is ubiquitous around here. Do you think I could convince anyone to take another gamble for someone who isn't even our kind?"

I watched him, dumbfounded. I half expected the rescue to already be underway.

"Ubiquitous means existing everywhere," Seraphina said to me.

"I know what ubiquitous means," I snapped back.

She shrugged. "Sorry. I guess that confused look is just how your face rests."

I gave her a stern look before turning back to Nur. "So, you're just going to let them torture him?"

He shook his head before I had even finished. "They didn't hurt Eren. We have no reason to believe they'd hurt Grant."

"But you can't know that for sure!"

"He's not our kind, Valerie. I can't risk the lives of our own—"

"Got it," I interrupted. I didn't care to hear Nur reiterate why Grant wasn't worth saving. "Then have me evoked, and I'll go get him myself."

Seraphina laughed.

"Have me evoked, and I'll do it myself," I repeated. "I know I can."

"And you know this, how?" Seraphina asked. "With all the prodigious research you've done?"

I gave her a weighted look. "I'm sorry about Candice, Seraphina. Honestly, I am. Though I never intended to harm her, I know that nothing I say can excuse what happened. But can't we set our differences aside for just one moment? An innocent person's life is on the line."

Seraphina didn't waiver. "If we listened to you, there would be more than one person's life at stake. You're right about one thing, though. Nothing you say can bring her back, so you might as well save your breath."

I folded my arms across my chest to keep from responding. Seraphina had every right not to accept my apology, but Grant needed me right now, and she stood in my way. If I allowed her to rile me up, it would only give Nur the impression that I hadn't thought this through. Nothing she had to say mattered, anyway. She wasn't the authority nor the glorified hybrid.

"If you have me evoked," I said to Nur, "then there won't be a need to put anyone else's life at risk."

Nur and Levi glanced at each other before setting their eyes on me again. They must not have expected me to know that whatever power I had laid dormant in me. Zoran was turning out to be a good friend to have.

Levi's silence irked me more than anything. If Cora was right, then he could override Nur's decision in an instant, but he merely stood there gawking at me.

Nur cleared his throat again. "We can't do that. It's far too dangerous."

"What *can* you do?"

He pressed his lips together, his expression sympathetic. He wasn't going to help me.

I cursed under my breath and stalked off down the path, biting back my anger. There they were, getting plastered while my brother was off, probably getting tortured by the Icis as we spoke. The *nerve* of them.

"Some help you were," I muttered to Eren, who trailed behind me.

He didn't say anything. Instead, he kept his eyes glued to the ground.

"I would go with you if I felt we had a chance," Cora said. "But you haven't been evoked, and I'd get wrecked before I could get close enough to do any actual harm."

"I know," I said, only to come to a halt in the middle of the hall. A surge of vertigo hit me, and I gripped the wall for support, but the world spun. The floor swayed beneath my feet....

Eren held me up. "Are you okay?"

"When was the last time you had something to drink?" Cora asked.

I looked back at her, but my eyes couldn't focus on her face. Everything was a blur. "I think I need to sit down."

"We're almost to the infirmary. You just need to walk a little bit more," Cora coaxed.

Eren positioned himself under my arm to keep me up as they guided me down the hall.

And that was the last thing I remembered.

I AWOKE TO FIND REN STANDING OVER ME WITH A disapproving look in her eyes, arms crossed over her chest. She droned on and on for what felt like hours about the importance of staying hydrated and insisted that she wouldn't always be there to nurse me back to health.

"Water is our life source. We're nothing without it," she repeated for the third time.

But she didn't understand how dangerous it could be— the damage it could do.

Ren had just begun to set up the chessboard for an afternoon game when the sheer lunacy of our situation compelled me to throw my face into my pillow and cry out, "Ugh. Nur is such a *dick*!"

"Is he?" Ren asked with a raised brow. "You can start us off, by the way."

"He's willing to cast aside an innocent man, and for what?" I asked, placing my white pawn up by one square. "Because Grant can't pull fire out of his ass like the rest of them? It's ridiculous."

"You know, not a lot of people know why I left Reota and settled here," she said, her eyes fixed on the board even after moving her black pawn, "but during the few weeks leading up to the Purity War, I was assaulted. He was, and perhaps still is, high in Calder's chain of command, which I think is why officials set him free. They said it was on account of a 'lack of evidence,' even though I left a clear gash across the man's neck after I slit his throat."

I sat up, having immediately matched the face to the injury, and drew my pillow tight over my chest. "Salil?"

She looked away for a moment as if to compose herself before waving for me to play my second move. "The Ignis didn't care that I wasn't one of them. They gave me a safe place to call home and accepted me for who I was. They treated me with a level of respect I had never been shown before—least of all by my own people—during a time that I could hardly stand to look at myself in the mirror. How do I tell myself that the innocence I held onto so casually before was now gone? I felt dirty, worthless, and violated. I couldn't imagine spending another second in my skin, and then the Ignis took me in. I don't know where I'd be if not for them. Sinking to the bottom of a lake somewhere, I imagine," she whispered before remembering she wasn't alone. She sniffed, wiping away a rogue tear. "Nur is a good man, Valerie," she said, "but even good people make mistakes."

I took a moment to consider my response. "So you agree he's making a mistake?"

Ren only pursed her lips, her queen knocking my king down with a light tap. "You truly are dreadful at this game. The last time I won by Fool's Mate was when little Sully came in with a nosebleed."

"I told you I only know how to play checkers."

"I wasn't about to snatch it away from the children for you."

I chuckled as I watched her put the pieces back in their places. And though I could tell she had already stuffed that awful memory deep into her subconscious mind, I rested my hand on hers and gave it a gentle squeeze.

"I'm so sorry, Ren."

In an effort to lighten the mood, she smiled, but it

didn't reach her eyes. "We'll find a way to help your brother. Just give us time."

Ren held me prisoner for two full days with Cora as my only contact with the outside world when she'd stop by with bundles of food. She brought along her sister Iri while dropping my dinner off on the second day, claiming she had been dying to meet me.

"She's never seen a Natura before," she explained.

Iri looked identical to Cora, only a younger version. But, unlike Fiametta, their hairless younger sibling, she actually spoke. I was glad I hadn't flinched at the sight of her eyes, finally having gotten used to them.

"Your hair is really pretty," Iri said.

I smiled at her. That was precisely what I needed to hear after feeling as though I were encased in filth for so long. "I like yours, too."

She shot a big toothy grin my way.

I laughed as she pulled out a piece of paper filled with questions about my life in the Origin. The first few were easy enough to answer: does the sun burn your skin if you're outside for too long? What is a hurricane? Have you ever seen a volcano?

But, as she reached the bottom of the list, her questions became more personal: what was it like growing up with humans? What was it like to have parents of different factions? Do your brothers wish they had been born first so they could've gotten your ethos?

By the end, my smile had faded. I struggled to answer Iri's remaining questions as I fought back the tears that threatened to spill at the mention of my family.

I wanted so badly to act, but every avenue appeared blocked. I hated my inability to protect my family. And I missed them. Even though Eren was with me now, I still felt terribly alone.

Cora picked up on my mood and told Iri to give it a rest. "I'm so sorry," she said to me. "I swear this kid will be the death of me."

"You said I could!" Iri complained.

"You're fine," I said to her, forcing a smile.

"See? I'm fine," Iri told Cora.

"You need to work on your social cues," Cora muttered back. She took a folded paper out of her pocket and handed it to me. "Fiametta drew this for you. Spot on, right?"

I chuckled. "It's like looking into a mirror."

Fiametta had drawn a wiggly stick figure with brown snake-like ringlets stemming in every direction of its head and two giant green orbs for eyes—a tiny smile beneath them. She even added a red mark on her forehead to account for my scar. Next to my portrait was another stick figure. Cora's. It warmed my heart.

Cora announced they couldn't stay for long. She had promised the girls she'd take them to the movie night hosted in the common room where *Toy Story 3* would play. I remembered a joke I had heard about it and relayed it to Iri.

"What did Woody say to Buzz?" I asked her.

Iri smiled, placing her finger to her chin as she thought. "Um, I don't know. What?"

"A lot," I said. "There were three movies."

Cora chuckled.

Iri's brows furrowed together. "I don't get it."

"Yeah, yeah, let's go. That joke is too smart for you," Cora teased before waving goodbye to me.

I missed her the moment she left. Even more so when I saw Ren resume her position guarding the exit. I would've liked to watch the movie, or any movie—anything to shake this feeling of utter uselessness off of me. I could only hope

they were right about the Icis not viewing Grant as a
threat. But I couldn't understand why they hadn't touched
a hair on Eren's head and, if anyone else did, they didn't
bother illuminating me.

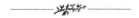

I SAT READING AN ALMOST DECADE-OLD ARTICLE IN A TEEN
magazine someone had left lying around when Levi and
Fintan walked into the room. I frowned at the sight of
Fintan, but what I found absolutely bizarre, even though
he had literally strangled me the first time we laid eyes on
each other, Levi's presence wasn't necessarily unwelcome.
And I couldn't understand why I didn't feel an inkling of
apprehension in his presence after the ordeal.

At this point, the fact that he chose to channel a mute
when I saw him last annoyed me more than the attempted
strangulation. Maybe because he only did so to determine if
I could be stopped, should I need to be. Or perhaps because
he and I had more in common than I would've liked—both
deemed a monster through no fault of our own.

But, Fintan, I could wholly do without. His beady black
eyes leered at me as though I were beneath him. And
though I just might be, I resented it.

Levi gave Ren, my unofficial prison guard, a deep
knowing nod before turning to me.

"You meant what you said about wanting to be
evoked," Levi began, though it wasn't a question—only a
recap of my earlier sentiments.

I nodded anyway.

"I can arrange that."

My eyes darted nervously to Ren and Fintan.

"Fintan won't breathe a word of this to anyone, and

Ren is all for the cause," Levi assured. "We'll need them to keep the others off our scent, so by the time they notice we're gone, it'll be too late to do anything about it. That is, if you're up for it."

"There aren't any Natura around to help me," I said.

He smiled. "You've made some chatty friends."

Fuck. Was I not supposed to know that?

"Lucky for you," he continued, "I've made a few of my own. One, in particular, will be of good use to us, but we have to get going. There's only about an hour left of the movie."

My heart soared with anticipation, only for it to nose-dive when Ren asked him to wait. She poured water into a cup and placed it in my hand.

"Drink," she ordered.

"I'm not really thirsty right now, but thank you," I said and handed it back to Ren as politely as I could when what I truly wanted to do was fling it at her. But she only nudged it back into my hand. *Rude.*

"Drink, Valerie," she insisted. "I don't think you understand what Levi's offer entails. I know how you feel about water, but we need to trust that you're able to set that aside before we risk slipping you out of here, only to have you change your mind at the lake. I won't be there to nurse you back to health if you faint again."

I blanched. "Why does it have to be the lake? Isn't there another way to get to the Origin?"

She shook her head. "I'm afraid not."

"*Fuck*," I cursed, pacing around the cot. I couldn't go back into the lake. I couldn't knowingly put myself back into that vat of acid. No sane person would.

It would be useless if I agreed, only to back out at the last minute, leaving Levi and me vulnerable so close to

Reota. But Grant needed me, and I couldn't help him in this state.

"She obviously can't do it," Fintan said, waving his hand at me in exasperation. "We're wasting our time here."

Levi reached out and held my arm to keep me still. "It'll only have to be once until we reach the Origin. The lake only burns for those who haven't been evoked to deter them. Once you're evoked, the lake can't hurt you. I'll be there to make sure we get through as fast as possible, but you have to tell me now. We're running out of time."

I bit my lip, tears welling up in my eyes. "It doesn't look like I have much of a choice," I said, finally. I eyed Ren scornfully as I knocked the water back and slammed the now empty cup onto the tray.

In the back of my mind, I knew she meant well. Way, way, back there. But I didn't care. Ren backed me into a corner that I desperately did not want to be in, making me appear weak in front of Levi and Fintan as I fought the violent urge to throw the water back up the entire time.

And, if a cup of water made me want to die, I couldn't imagine how I'd feel facing the acidic lake for a second time.

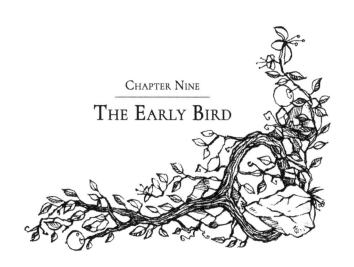

CHAPTER NINE

THE EARLY BIRD

"IT'LL BE OKAY. YOU CAN DO THIS," LEVI WHISPERED.

We stood by the edge of the lake. Their mock sun had long since scurried off, and the mock wind blew so cold it carried razor blades, which, in turn, made it impossible to breathe. I pressed my palm against my tightening chest to the point of pain as adrenaline shot through my system, hoping the pressure would slow my palpitating heart. It didn't.

Levi positioned himself in front of me, placing his hands on my shoulders. "We're going to run in and, I'm not going to lie to you, it's going to hurt like hell, but I'll be there. I'm going to pull you to the bottom, so it takes you first. Don't fight the roots, and it'll be over before you know it. Once on the other side, I'll get you out."

The lake's inky water sloshed around behind him, taunting me.

"Valerie, look at me. Look at me," he said, veering my eyes away from the water until I met his gaze. The warmth from his hands felt remarkable against my frozen cheeks. "I'll get you out. I promise."

To my surprise, his words and soft expression actually alleviated some of my anxiety.

I marveled at the stunning clarity and vivid hue of his eyes and wished we were diving into them instead. It baffled me that theoretically, Levi shared the same shade as Nerio and the other Icis. I refused to believe it.

I couldn't pinpoint exactly what it was about Levi that radiated honesty and security, but I trusted he would get me through this, so I nodded to show that I was ready. Before I could change my mind, he took my hand and pulled me along as he barreled into the lake.

The acid spread faster than I could grow accustomed to the deeper we went, an inconceivable notion to begin with. The pain was so debilitating it had me panting and pulling against Levi's hand so that I could rush back to shore, but he refused to let go. Before I had a chance to process how far we really were, he drew me against his chest and dove us into the darkness.

I thrashed against him, but he had one arm encircling me, effectively pinning my arms at my sides while the other propelled us forward. But, I hadn't had a chance to suck in my last breath and had begun to run out of the bit I had.

My panic compelled me to open my eyes, which only made things worse. A lesson I had come to learn but not apply—as one does. I couldn't see anything through the blackness but could feel Levi's exertion against my body as he swam deeper into the lake with me in tow until my leg hit something solid.

Levi gripped me with both hands now and pushed me into the lakebed. Something gave way and wrapped itself around my abdomen, pulling me in.

Finally, I thought. *Just end it.*

I PUSHED MYSELF UPWARDS UNTIL MY HEAD BROKE FREE from the water's surface. I focused my thoughts on the fact that I was more than halfway done with the excruciating task as I took in huge gulps of air, paddling frantically to the edge of the lake. Then, something grabbed my legs, spreading them before hitting my pelvic region.

I screamed, squirming until my hands reached down and felt hair. I stopped fighting when I realized it was Levi propping me over his shoulders. I held onto his head, a bit too tightly, as his arms wrapped themselves around my calves to secure me. Soon, my shoulders and chest broke free, and then he liberated my entire body. I looked down to see Levi trudging up the shore, and I sagged against the back of his head in absolute relief.

It's over, I rejoiced. *I'll never have to experience that ever again!*

We reached the shore, where Levi pried me off his shoulders and onto my feet, but he still didn't let go. Instead, he pulled me against his chest and held me, running his hand down the length of my back, and it took me a while to realize why. I shook like a leaf, and his arms were the only thing keeping me from crumbling to the ground. The warmth emanating from his core drew me closer to him, and I allowed myself to burrow my face into his chest.

"You're okay. I've got you. You're okay," Levi said, over and over into my hair. "You did so well."

When my shaking subsided, the only thing left was a lingering sense of mortification. I was now hyper-aware of Levi's body against mine and embarrassed at just how much I enjoyed it there.

I stepped away from him, spinning to face the opposite direction. On the off chance he could see the blood rushing to my cheeks, I pretended to slap some sense into myself a few times so he'd associate the slaps with their redness before turning back to him. "Off to see the wizard we go!" I said and cringed at how shrill my voice sounded.

He chuckled, his expression more amused than anything. "Down the yellow brick road."

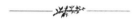

LEVI ANNOUNCED WE'D BE STOPPING BY THE IGNIS' BASE IN the Origin, which happened to be a plain cabin a few yards away from the lake, to change into dry clothes before making our way to the road. Levi, very gentleman-like, advised he'd change outside to give me privacy as I donned on a fresh set of tan clothing. Now, why they insisted it all be brown, I had no clue. Personally, I would have preferred colors marked with dust over a seemingly dustless tan outfit, but to each his own.

Once dressed, he unlocked a parked black Jeep close to the road and motioned for me to hop in.

I wondered idly how they made money to afford these things. An Ignis couldn't last long in the Origin without their telltale eyes giving them away. Could they have some sort of pact with the Natura or Ventus who lived out here?

I couldn't see that happening. Remembering Nur's words when I asked him to send someone after Grant, it didn't seem likely they'd place that level of responsibility and trust on another faction.

"We don't exactly 'work' for the money, Valerie," Levi said when I asked him.

I gaped at him. "You mean, you *steal* it?"

He eyed me incredulously. "Did you honestly believe we held nine-to-fives to pay for all of this?"

"Well, no," I laughed, "but I didn't think I was living with a pack of thieves either."

I yearned to ask Levi for a minor detour, but a sobering fact gave me pause. I wanted to see my father more than anything, but if he spun a story for me like he did Eren, then perhaps it wouldn't be such a good idea to be seen. Anyway, we didn't have that luxury with Grant being held by the Icis, so I would have to save my questions for another time. I only hoped I could survive till then.

I opened the glove compartment and found a collection of dark-tinted sunglasses.

Of course, the Ignis couldn't possibly make the runs without them.

I lifted a pair with a whopping set of lenses and tried them on.

"Those look nice on you," Levi said.

I turned to him and smiled. "Thanks."

I had thought of switching to a sleeker pair, but I closed the compartment and secured the bug-eyed frames instead. Then, I proceeded to open the sun visor and flip the mirror's cover to primp the rest while remaining as nonchalant as possible. I fixed my hair's parting and pushed my tresses, still damp from the lake, over my shoulders to add volume, only to sigh as I looked back at my reflection.

I hope I'm funny today.

I perked up when Levi announced we had to stop for gas. I craved to eat anything other than bread, cheese, and chicken. So much so that I could already taste the saltiness of the Pringles and the sweetness of the powdery donuts I planned to snag, and it made my mouth water.

I took one last look at myself before waltzing in and chuckled. "We look like we escaped a cult in these clothes."

"Haven't we?" Levi asked.

We were still laughing as we made our way to the counter, where a balding middle-aged attendant asked Levi where we came from conversationally.

"The Heaven's Gate compound down the road," I answered.

We broke into laughter again and couldn't stop. Levi apologized to him when he finally managed to reign it in, only to realize he had forgotten to note the number of our gas pump.

I ran out, recorded the number mentally, and called it out to him before skipping to the shelves. I grabbed a gluttonous amount of snacks for the road, along with two of the comically tiny magic eight balls they sold at the counter. Levi insisted it was too much but folded when he took in my sullen expression.

WE CAME TO A STOP BY A HEAVILY WOODED AREA AFTER having driven into a dead-end road, and I followed Levi out of the Jeep as he led us through the woods. It was the beginning of May, nearly the start of summer, yet it was still fifty degrees out. It looked like I had grown accustomed to the warmth of the Ignis cave.

But, as we descended deeper into the woods, I came to appreciate the temperature. At least it wasn't cold enough for snow to stick to the ground. The trek would have been significantly more taxing if we had to haul through the slush while it wet our socks. We weren't necessarily dressed for a hike.

The trees grew tall enough to brush the sky but not enough to keep the sun's rays from shining through the cracks, leaving behind dancing flickering shadows over the moss-covered rocks and flora. I brushed my fingers over the rough, cracked ridges of tree bark, listening to the birds calling in the distance and the trees creaking and groaning as they swayed in the wind.

Levi broke branches and swatted away spiderwebs to clear the way for me, but he didn't speak. I followed, admiring his forceful push into the woods and the breathtaking scenery when a deep grumbling broke the silence. Levi stopped ahead and placed his finger over his lips to signal me to be quiet.

A rustling came from the right, and when I turned to the sound, I came face to face with a bear. And it stared right back at us.

"Shit," Levi cursed, clutching my arm to keep me still as he positioned himself directly between the bear and me.

I covered my mouth with my palm and took a step back. I had never seen a bear in person before. I had heard stories of sightings all around Fairbanks but never caught sight of one myself apart from on television, of course. And it surely did not do their size or greatness any justice. This bear must have been six feet tall on all fours. A total monster if it were to stand on its hind legs. I looked around us, attempting to map out the easiest escape, but what I found easy for us would be equally easy for the bear. I had read about their ability to climb trees, so I chucked that idea out of my mind. I hoped Levi had come up with a better one. Or any.

The moment the thought crossed my mind, Levi raised his arm towards the bear, and a bright blue flame materialized in his palm.

Tell me he doesn't plan on setting the bear on fire . . .

"Don't! Don't kill 'em!" So yelled a stout, older woman running at us from our left, her arms waving wildly over her head.

Levi sighed a breath of relief. "You can't have them

wandering around like that, Hestia. A hunter could've passed by here and seen him."

Astonishingly, the old woman walked straight up to the bear, patting him on his shoulder. "It's a lass," she corrected in a heavy Scottish accent. "Wasn't a hunter that was 'bout to kill the gal now, was it?"

Levi ignored the question and steered me out from behind him. "Hestia, I brought someone I'd like you to meet."

I stood awkwardly between them, not wanting to get any closer to the bear, even though she seemed as docile as a dog now.

Hestia eyed me lazily for a moment before her eyes widened with realization. "What in the heavens . . . " Her voice trailed off as she closed the space between us, her gaze darting from my umber hair to my jade-shaded eyes in rapid succession before fixing on Levi. "What have ya done?"

"It wasn't my doing," Levi said. "I'll explain on the way to your cabin."

"No, lad," Hestia objected. "I'm workin' with a Natura, and this lassie can't be seen by a soul if she plans to carry on breathin'."

Levi gave her a half-hearted shrug. "I wouldn't be here if we had any other choice."

Hestia paused to examine me, searching for something in my expression, though I could hardly imagine what, so I merely stood there like a kid who's confessed to wetting their bed.

Innocent. Confused. Pathetic.

Finally, she shook her head, mumbled something to herself, and trudged off, waving impatiently to signal us to follow.

LEVI AND HESTIA STOOD ARGUING APART FROM A MODEST wooden cabin where Hestia lived. I sat on one of the slated rocks that circled a campfire, waiting for the verdict, as Levi attempted to convince Hestia to evoke me, while Hestia tried to persuade Levi of its needlessness. I considered weighing in but decided to stay in my lane—fearing I'd only come off as power-hungry. So instead, I snapped twigs I collected from the ground into smaller bits and flung them into the fire. The bear had wandered off midway into our trek, much to my relief, but I couldn't quite relax knowing she still lurked around in the woods somewhere.

A man stepped out of the cabin. Cute, with an adorably upturned nose. He glanced at Hestia and Levi, who were incapable of noticing anything amid their argument, and then turned to me. He smiled, revealing a set of dimples, and sat opposite me by the fire.

"Hey," he said.

I chuckled. It was the most ordinary interaction I'd had in months. "Hi."

He leaned forward, giving me a once-over, before finally making the connection. "Oh shit. You're not—"

"Yes," I interrupted. "Yes, I am."

He raised his brows and nodded slowly. With his brown hair and eyes, he must have been the Natura Hestia had referred to before. He shot another glance at the two quarreling before settling back to me. "So, are we training together?"

I shrugged. "That has yet to be determined."

He didn't reach out to shake my hand. He only smiled. "Well, my name's George. What's yours?"

"George? Like, G-E-O-R-G-E?" I asked, stifling a laugh.

"Yep."

"Hestia, Leviathan, and *George*," I mused.

"It means earth-worker," he said, giving me a lopsided grin. "You still haven't told me yours."

"I'm Valerie."

His brows furrowed together. "No. Your real name," he insisted.

Before I could question what he meant, Hestia strode over to us, grunting all the while. She had waved the white flag. "If we do this, we do it my way," she said. "Yer to stay until I feel yer got a grip on yer ethos. Deal?"

I stood, extending my hand out to her. "Deal."

She shot a dubious look at it. "Don't lay a finger on folk you don't know. Consider that yer first lesson."

HESTIA HAD LEVI DRIVE FOR TWO HOURS BEFORE SHE decided we were far enough away, declaring the area had to be sufficiently secluded so any damage wouldn't be noticed immediately.

George stayed behind for safety reasons, which did nothing to abate my anxiety.

She settled for a bare stretch of land, with only small bushes and rocks scattered sparingly around. As I watched Hestia scan the area for any other obstructions, the severity of what we were about to do finally registered with me. Was it too late to run?

She asked that I lie on my back in the center of the clearing, and I did so with a growing sense of apprehension—biting my lip to reign in my nerves.

Levi stepped forward and placed a hand on Hestia's

shoulder. "I'll take care of it," he said.

Hestia nodded and strode out of view.

Levi knelt beside me. "Listen, Valerie," he said. "When she starts to recite the words, it'll trigger your ethos. Your body will tell you to release it—to completely lose yourself. But I need you to fight that instinct. Otherwise, we're as good as dead."

"That's encouraging," I muttered, remembering Zoran's description of the damage brought on after Levi's evocation. I couldn't fathom the thought of seriously hurting anyone, and I didn't have much faith in my ability to control much of anything anymore. I could be jeopardizing the lives of everyone in the vicinity—Levi and Hestia included. And we had no guarantee I would even be enough to save Grant. "I don't know if this is such a good idea anymore," I admitted in a whisper.

"You can do it, Valerie," he said. "You've overcome far worse."

Had I, though? Because it seemed to me like I was still smack dab in the middle of it all. But, I shook out my hands and closed my eyes anyway as I listened to Hestia chant in a language I had never heard before. Whether I felt prepared or not, Hestia had initiated the ritual, and my body had already started to itch with anticipation.

Levi gave my hand a tight squeeze before I sensed him leave my side.

As I listened to Hestia, it hit me that I was experiencing something ancient and powerful, a ritual that had been done for thousands of years before I even existed. The weight of her words pressed down onto my chest like a ton of bricks. Although I had no idea what Hestia said, the quiescent power inside me knew only too well, and I could already feel my fingers and toes tingle as my body responded to her words.

With every passing word, a latch inside me came loose. The fragment that escaped became restless with its newfound freedom. As Levi's words reminded me, I attempted to subdue them, but it became increasingly difficult as more and more latches came undone.

As I struggled to herd them, I realized I could only faintly hear Hestia over a thunderous commotion all around me. I wasn't doing as thorough a job as I thought.

The fragments were downright unmanageable, and I prayed for some sort of intermission, but Hestia didn't waiver. I clenched my hands into fists as I strained to hold onto each and every one of them, but it was as though I were playing a game of fifty-two pick up where they expected me to catch every card in one go. Naturally, a few would escape my grasp. But, this was not a game. I couldn't just laugh it off if I failed. So, I focused my energy on quartering them.

I tensed, my back arching, as I fought to reign the fragments in—sweating profusely as I fought against them. But, they were stubborn. They didn't want to cooperate. I gritted my teeth, took a deep breath, and held on until, finally, the fragments began to settle into their new surroundings—the excitement of being set free having waned.

And now, though my eyes remained shut, I could plainly see them. The countless fragments that made up my ethos buzzed around my core like a swarm of bees, and, like bees, they seemed to have a hive mind. They acted in service of each other, in favor of *me*.

I lifted my hand as a test, and I could feel the fragments eagerly rush to my fingertips with anticipation.

My ethos had relinquished its control and molded itself to me, readying to emerge once again at my command.

CHAPTER TEN

DARK HORSE

I COULDN'T UNDERSTAND WHY THEY WERE AGAINST THE idea of my evocation until Hestia ceased her chanting.

The difference? Indisputable. I could feel the power coursing through my veins beyond what I could see, feel, or touch. Even if I had no idea how to use it yet, I could sense it waiting, biding its time until it could resurface once again.

Certainly, not the same body I spent the previous twenty-six years in.

I felt a slight pressure on my hand and heard Levi's smooth voice above me. "Nod if you can hear me."

I did while gradually opening my eyes only to see him peering down at me.

"Apart from a minor quake and a few stripped trees, the damage was minimal. You did a phenomenal job," Levi whispered. "But you must feel weak," he added, a little louder to be sure Hestia could hear. Before I could respond, he rested his fingers softly on my lips to hint at silence—a knowing look in his eyes.

I blinked slowly to show I understood . . . sort of.

Levi knew I didn't feel weak in the slightest, quite the opposite. I felt like I could singlehandedly take on an entire army. So that could only mean that this feeling wasn't typical. It could only mean that Hestia, and everyone else for that matter, couldn't know the full extent of the power resting inside of us.

He nodded. I didn't know if he did so to acknowledge my answer or encourage my ruse because a more critical thought bubbled its way to the surface.

"I really killed Candice, didn't I?" I asked him, my voice barely above a whisper.

Pointed silence.

I squeezed my eyes shut, struggling to push the image of Candice's lifeless body out of my mind. Convinced that I couldn't have done something so horrific with a simple touch, I detached myself from the memory. But now, I awoke only too aware of the energy coursing through me, too aware of what it was capable of.

I really *killed* someone.

Levi brushed his hand over my hair. "You were afraid, and your body defended you," he said, a profound sadness clouding his features. "I'll do everything in my power to help you, Valerie. You will *not* end up like me."

HESTIA TESTED ME FOR AN ENTIRE MONTH. MUCH LONGER than Levi and I had initially projected. But, as much as I wanted to rush back into the Oasis, storm Reota, and rescue Grant, I had promised Hestia that I would leave only once adequately equipped to handle myself, and I intended to keep that promise.

We knew my abilities would be heightened compared

to other Natura's based on what we knew of Levi. His signature blue flames burned considerably hotter than the fires of the Ignis, and we believed his recessive Icis genes brought about his immunity to fire, keeping his body in a constant state of hydration.

So far, we discovered I had an affinity to mold the earth around me. I noticed it worked best with direct contact, so I chose to work barefoot. Unlike Levi, my ethos required I communicate with the living, so the closer I was to them, the clearer the connection, so to speak.

When I planted my feet on the ground, I could sense the grass, trees, and earth waiting for instruction; as though we shared the same mind—my thoughts ran intertwined with theirs. I didn't need to bark orders at them; it was not that sort of relationship. Instead, I would request what I needed from them, and they seemed only too happy to oblige. We worked together, cohesively—a symbiotic relationship. If I needed shelter, I could coax the trees and plants to shield me. If I needed a weapon, I could summon a sharpened root from deep underground to do my bidding.

Hestia and Levi watched as I glided through her lessons with entirely different reactions.

Levi watched with widening eyes, seemingly in awe and absolutely captivated with how the earth moved so effortlessly around me. Every so often, his excitement made him burst with spontaneous laughter, and I'd flash him a smile in return.

Hestia's expression, on the other hand, remained guarded. At times she looked impressed, and at others, she looked . . . concerned. Finally, I decided to tone down the full extent of my gift. At least, around anyone that wasn't Levi since it would only make them uneasy.

"An ethos runs on emotions, but those tend to be fleeting," Hestia explained. "So, yer must channel an emotion that lasts to adequately fuel it. But too strong of an emotion will wear yerself to a frazzle and leave ya without the strength to carry on."

"So basically, it's all a big balancing act?"

"Precisely. Yer ethos is a muscle, and muscles tire. Yer must exercise it. Train it."

Hestia worked on keeping my thoughts focused on what I needed from the earth. She asked me to run while simultaneously calling on the roots to lift me up, but I kept toppling over the confused tangle beneath me.

"Yer falling into yer own trap, lass! Pace yerself!"

"I'm trying," I insisted through gritted teeth. "It's not as easy as you think it is."

I had trouble focusing every now and then with the pressure to excel weighing so heavily on my shoulders because I couldn't simply meet their expectations if I was to be of any use to the cause. I needed to surpass them.

Levi's unabashed staring didn't do much to help my focus either.

"Never said it was easy," Hestia said. "But I know ya can do it. Failin' only means yer playin'."

I glanced down just in time to see Hestia's soft and nurturing expression—her earth-brown eyes kind. The old woman risked everything to help us, and I'd be damned if I let her down.

TWO WEEKS IN, HESTIA PRESENTED ME WITH A POUCH OF seeds, which she described as the bullets to my proverbial "gun." I regarded the trees and plants around me with a newfound reverence and admiration for their uniqueness and wide range of utility, like the ostrich ferns and horsetails, which were used to soften a landing. The spruces and the aspens were perfect for concealment. The alders and black cottonwoods were prime for climbing. Yarrow could stop blood flow from wounds, and the paper birch's roots were sharp enough to pierce the skin and an organ or two.

We found it helped to use species native to the area, as a Sitka spruce required less support growing in Alaska than a kapok tree native to Mexico.

I paid close attention to this lesson. I studied all throughout the night until sunshine spilled onto the wooden floors, fully aware it would be instrumental to my survival.

"YOU CAN CONTROL ANIMALS?" I ASKED HESTIA DURING my lesson on poisonous plants. I really hoped I had guessed correctly because a family of moose had ambled over just then to nibble on the horsetails I had grown. I had never thought to be afraid of a herbivore, but these beasts weren't the size of reindeer—they were colossal creatures that towered several feet above us.

"We have an understandin'," she said, completely unfazed by their presence. "The Natura don't control, lass. We work hand in hand with the livin'."

I nodded. It was precisely how I felt with the earth beneath my feet. But just as I had gotten used to the moose, we heard a rustling in the trees above us, and I yelped in surprise when a *panther* leaped out of the alder and strolled over to me.

"Oh, hush! It's only Eika," Hestia said as its bright green eyes bore into mine, "and it looks like she's taken a likin' to ya. She's been followin' us since the moment yer arrived."

Unlike my brief interaction with Hestia's pet bear and moose, I didn't necessarily fear this animal. Even though she was most definitely a carnivore, she didn't approach me with any apprehension, as she would her prey or an adversary. Instead, she came to me as though we were good friends who hadn't seen each other in a while.

Much to my amazement, she brushed her head against my hip like an unassuming housecat and purred. Without thinking, I pet her behind the ear and felt her lean into my hand, making me beam from ear to ear and giggle for the first time in months.

So is this what it's like to be a Disney princess? I could get used to this.

"DO WE LIKE THESE?" I ASKED THE BOYS, MOTIONING TO A bowl of peaches. The sun had set, signaling the end of another day of training which left me drained and starved.

George shook his head. "Not ripe yet."

I looked down at them, noticing the slight green tinge on their skin. I placed my fingers against them, focused on how much I yearned for peaches, and gradually the green tinge turned to orange and yellow. "I think they're good now."

Levi walked around the pit, picked one up, and spun it in his hand. "Nifty," he said, smiling at me—an oh so lovely smile. He grabbed the rest and placed them onto the cutting board, where he began to prepare the fruit for us.

"Do you want to help start a new fire?" George asked Levi after a fierce gust of wind blew out our previously existing one, leaving behind a billowing pillar of smoke. George watched him expectedly, annoyed with Levi's choice of labor, but, considering Levi could summon fire with a snap of his fingers, I could understand his frustration.

"You seem to have a good grip on it," Levi answered, not even bothering to look up.

I elbowed Levi. "Behave," I whispered.

He shrugged, but I could see the corner of his mouth pinch into a smirk.

George rolled his eyes before stomping off into the woods in search of firewood.

I walked over to Hestia, who sat sharpening a knife. "George mentioned something when I first got here about Valerie not being my 'real' name," I said. "Why do you think he said that?"

She stopped, placing the blade on her knee. "Well, 'cause it's not."

"How could you possibly know that?"

"Valerie isn't a Natura name, nor is it a Ventus one. So Levi and I did some diggin', and we figured it out," she said.

I glanced at Levi, who didn't look up as he cubed the fruit, before returning my attention back to her. "Out with it, Hestia. The suspense is killing me."

"Yer name is Valterra," she said plainly.

"*Valterra?*"

"We checked the book," Levi said. He had finished dicing and flung the knife at the board, impaling the wood with a loud thud. "It took us a while to put two and two together, but it helped that your parents chose the closest human equivalents. We believe Eren's real name to be Erion, Grant's to be Gaothaire, and yours to be Valterra."

"Valterra," I repeated, trying to get a feel for it. It certainly packed a punch. "And our last name?"

"We have no use for last names," Levi said. "Lineages and bloodlines don't play a part in our world like they do in yours. Here, you're given a name based on your individual importance and power. They say what's chosen can signify what the child will live up to be—take Zoran's, for example. Zoran means 'light of dawn,' and he's foreseen to be our savior."

My eyes widened. "We're doomed."

Levi chuckled as he divvied up the fruit among us.

Three large rocks already encircled the pit, but there were four of us, so I looked around and noticed a slightly smaller, more jagged rock a few feet away. I attempted to push it towards our cluster, but it just wouldn't budge.

"Step back," Levi said from behind me, a small smile playing on his lips. "I'm gonna try a different trick."

"What's the trick?" I asked, brushing the dirt off my palms.

"I'm going to push it really, really hard."

I laughed. "I wish I would've thought of that."

I watched his body respond to the physical exertion as the rock, being no match for Levi, toppled over and over again until it met up with the others. I could see his muscles outlined through his shirt, the sweat of the day's work making it cling to him, and I bit my lip. Why did I find his casual use of brute strength so absurdly attractive?

Levi dusted off the rock before gesturing for me to have a seat, and I had to take a deep breath before settling onto the boulder. I didn't realize how touch-deprived I had become, but I needed to reel myself back in before I made a fool of myself.

George returned and began piling his findings into the pit. Once he had, he took out a match from his pocket, but before George could light it, Levi raised his hand in the pit's direction, and his blazing blue fire shot out and into the pit—growing as it consumed the firewood.

George sighed, realizing he had spent the past twenty

minutes working in vain, and flicked his unlit match into the flames.

WE HUDDLED AROUND THE CRACKLING FIRE, WATCHING Levi's blue flames turn the woodpile into soot and ash, entirely at ease. We could have come across as an average, run-of-the-mill family out camping for the Fourth of July weekend to anyone that saw us. The hint of normalcy comforted me so much that I handled taking a small sip from the water canteen relatively well when Levi passed it my way, nearly forgetting why I ever feared it at all. That is, until the water touched my lips, reminding me all over again.

George asked Levi about the conditions in which the Ignis lived, sparking a full-blown discussion between the two, so I took the liberty of scooting closer to Hestia since I had a few questions of my own.

When I reached her, she offered me a grape bunch, but I waved them away with a chuckle. "I'm not trying to pinch fruits off your plate," I assured her. "I only wanted to thank you. I know you're taking a huge risk with helping us, and, well . . ." But, I fell silent, at a loss for how to adequately express my gratitude to a woman who took me in when she had every reason to turn me away.

I took a deep breath, searching for the right words, when she stopped me.

"When ya witness injustice, Valerie, it is yer duty to act. I may be but a wee shadow of me former self, so perhaps I'd be a fool to fight, but if I ken give ya the tools to succeed in my stead, then I will."

"That's quite noble of you. If only everyone thought that way, then all would be right in the world."

"Aye," Hestia agreed, laughing. "But till then, we decent folk must stick together."

I smiled at her, then focused on plucking the lint off my jeans.

"What else is on yer mind, lass?" she asked in a gentler tone.

"Why did they create us? The gods, I mean. Sometimes, I get the impression we've only been put on this earth to suffer, but then, what the hell is the point in that?"

"Ah," she sighed. "You've reached the fundamental question." Hestia popped a grape into her mouth, tilting her head towards the stars. "That question has givin' me countless sleepless nights and, even at my auld age, I'm no closer to an answer. But do we truly need a reason, Valerie?"

I followed her gaze. Out here in the woods, so far from civilization, the stars cluttered the sky—vying for our attention. With no electricity to drown them out, they sparkled so brightly they almost blended into one another. A night like this one made me wish I had bothered to learn constellations. "It would be nice to have an idea, though," I insisted. "Not just to quench our curiosity, but to steer us down the right path."

"Yer won't know till yer swept up into the arms of yer creator, but I believe the true test is whether you ken get there on yer own."

I peered back at her only to see her smiling at me, and she winked.

"How did you come to live here all alone, Hestia?" George asked.

We turned at the sound of his voice to see both men watching us. I wasn't sure if I imagined it, but the distance between them seemed to grow exponentially. Their conversation mustn't've gone as well as ours had.

Hestia's entire demeanor changed. She didn't answer right away, but the words came out in a rush when she did. "My kin were killed when we answered the call from the Ignis."

Her response took us by surprise. No one expected her answer to be quite so intense.

"What call?" George asked.

I glared at him from across the firepit. If it weren't for the fact that he sat on the other side of a raging fire, I would've given him a swift kick to the shin for his tactless questions.

"After Levi's evocation, it was bedlam. Aiden was but a wee lad then, so they appointed his mother, Cinaed, as authority till he came of age. She was a good friend to me and my Lachlan . . ." Hestia's voice trailed off, and her expression dulled. She shook herself free of a memory before continuing. "Cinaed asked us to help 'em, and we couldn't say no, knowin' what we did. But the Icis had prepared for that fight long before any law had been broken."

We ate quietly after that, Hestia's bleak mood having naturally spread to the rest of us.

I wiped the tears that formed in the corners of my eyes, flustered by our less-than-ideal situation. So many had been lost then, and I couldn't help but wonder how many more would be lost in the fight looming over us. How was I supposed to tip the scale when I was only one person?

But I figured I could either fixate on our meager prospects and potentially psych myself out, or I could suck it up and roll with the punches. I deemed the first option counterproductive and settled for the second. Why set myself up for failure when I have never had any trouble getting there on my own?

We had an array of fruits to consume for dinner that

night: berries, melons, grapes, bananas, and now peaches —thanks to me. Though none of these fruit-bearing trees were native to Alaska, they grew marvelously under the guidance of my ethos. After weeks of living off cheese and meat, it was a welcome change.

Levi made sure the water canteen always made its way back to me and remained vigilant on the off chance I tried to pull a fast one on him. I didn't intend to, but I still took my sips with caution. My pulse raced with every drop, but I couldn't afford to faint again, so I consumed fruits with high water content, like watermelons and strawberries, to compensate for my sparing water breaks. I noticed my brain didn't particularly associate them with water, so I didn't physically react to them.

I couldn't trick my mind into bathing, though. Drinking water affected a concentrated area, making it much easier to regulate, and, as Ren loved to remind me, I needed it to survive. On the other hand, bathing required a full-body encounter that could surely be left to my discretion—and it was a no from me. I could only go as far as dragging a soaped-up washcloth over myself.

Not ideal, but not terrible either.

Once I finished my plate, I peered into the bowl of prepared fruit, searching for more peaches, and didn't find any. Levi must've been watching me since he scooped up the three remaining peach slices off his plate and placed them onto mine.

I smiled up at him. They were his favorite, too.

"Eat up," he said. "Hestia will be busy working with George tomorrow, so I'll be the one training you."

Now, that was exciting news.

HESTIA AND GEORGE RETIRED TO THE CABIN A WHILE AFTER dinner, leaving me alone with Levi, and my cheeks turned pink with anticipation. I detected a sort of magnetism between us, and I didn't quite care what caused it, but I knew something similar stirred within him, too.

I sat next to him, our backs against the trunk of a cottonwood, as he fiddled with twigs, and he looked almost nervous. I bit my lip to hide my smirk.

"What are you thinking about?" I asked.

"Tonight, I was reminded of things that I prefer never to think about," he said, breaking off a piece of the twig in his hand and flinging it into his blue flames. It disintegrated instantly.

My frisky mood vanished in a flash. His mind was far from where I hoped it would be, and I was ashamed to have hoped for that at all. There were far more pressing matters at hand besides my libido. "Your parents?"

He didn't answer, but his hands formed tight fists around the remaining twig until it snapped.

I turned to face him, placing my hands over his fists. "I'm sorry you had to go through that, Levi, but I don't pity you," I said, choosing my words with care. "I pity lost causes, and that's not you."

Levi's gaze flickered from his flames to my eyes, and I could swear the air sizzled around us.

The intensity in his stare made me tense. I hadn't had a chance to prepare, to set my poker face, and now he saw right through me.

But what if Levi didn't like what he saw? What if all he saw was a mess of a woman he didn't want to clean up? What then?

Levi lifted his hand and, at a tentative pace, closed the space between us—as if attempting to gauge my reaction. When I didn't object, his fingers trailed down my cheek to my neck, where his hand once clutched, but this time, with a warm and feathery touch that made me shiver. "How can you be so kind to me after everything I've done?"

I frowned. I couldn't be sure if Levi referred to what he did to me all those months ago or what he'd done as a whole, but I figured I'd answer as though he meant the latter since I couldn't quite understand the first, myself. "You couldn't help it," I said.

"Not my evocation, sure. But every subsequent action that followed was a conscious decision on my part. My hands are stained red with the blood of hundreds of both Icis and Ignis, Valerie . . . and that didn't just go away after I chose to side with the Ignis."

"You were only defending yourself."

"All I did was prove them right," he whispered, shaking his head. "And now you're left to suffer the consequences of *my* actions."

"I've made my fair share of mistakes, Levi. Don't burden yourself by taking them on, too. They've gotten used to having you around, and that's a good sign, isn't it?"

"The Ignis tolerate me. But, they don't accept me."

"Well, you don't exactly exude an air of approachability with your devil-may-care attitude," I teased, nudging him.

He smiled, but it didn't reach his eyes. "I'd prefer to be alone if the alternative is engaging in conversation with people I don't care about."

"Then what are we talking about here?"

"With the exception of Nur, I have no interest in bonding with any of those people. But I fear because of that, I've burned the bridge that would have allowed you to bond with them," he said, reaching for another bundle of twigs only to shunt them away with a violent wave of his hand. "And I just can't stand the way they look at you."

Both his reaction and his words stunned me. All this time, I assumed Levi sat reflecting on his own miserable situation when really he sat contemplating mine—and blaming himself for it. I sat back against the trunk of the tree, nestling against his side.

He tensed but lifted his arm a moment later and rested it over my shoulders.

"Don't worry about me," I whispered. "I'm exactly where I want to be."

Levi sighed, drawing me closer against his chest, and I felt a slight pressure on my head.

His lips? I thought—and secretly hoped.

Eika plopped down from her hiding spot and wiggled herself against my legs. We sat in silence, watching the panther breathe in and out until her adorable, not-so-little face went slack with sleep. Of course, I followed suit soon after.

In Levi's arms and with Eika by my side, I slept dream-lessly for the first time in months.

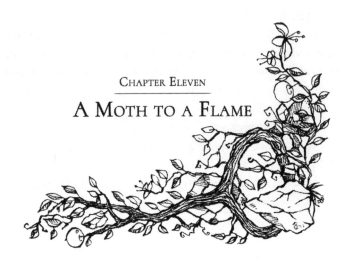

Chapter Eleven

A Moth to a Flame

I AWOKE ALMOST GIDDY WITH ANTICIPATION ON THE HEELS OF the night before. Partly because the first thing I saw was Levi's soft smile as my head rested on his lap, and partly because I knew I'd have a full day to spend with him. And *just* him.

I had spent the last couple of months learning as much as I could from Hestia while at the same time being compelled to hold back. But, how was I expected to teach myself boundaries if I wasn't allowed to explore the magnitude of my abilities?

Fortunately, with Levi, I didn't need to do the same.

Levi and I wandered into the woods, where he had me kneel over a patch of dirt beside him. He placed his palm over the soil and summoned his signature blue fire. It blazed quietly under his palm, even taking licks at him, and though he didn't react to the flames, it still jarred me to see.

"I want you to grow something here," Levi said. "Anything."

My forehead puckered. "Inside the fire, you mean?"

"Yes."

I watched the flames with what I thought were reasonable reservations but placed my hands into the ground, anyway. I imagined a seedling sprouting from underneath and heard a slight pop and sizzle. The seedling had grown only to be incinerated instantly.

"I can't," I said, my shoulders sagging.

"Don't forget you're part Ventus. Think of a way to create a barrier between the plant and my fire."

I mulled that over for a moment before digging my hands deeper into the soil. I pictured a small exclusive vacuum surrounding my sprout, and finally, we heard the pop but no sizzle.

"Do you feel that?" Levi asked. "It's growing!"

"That's what she said."

"Valerie," he protested.

"Yes. Yes, I feel that," I said, giggling, and Levi joined in. The sprout had emerged in what looked like a bubble and, since fire can't survive without oxygen, the absence of air prevented the flames from reaching her.

"Were you always able to do this?" I asked him. "Even a little before you were evoked?"

"Oh, yeah," he said. "If I got really angry or sad, I'd find that the same strange blue fire would crop up all around me. Nothing on command, though, until after my evocation."

I nodded. "Same here. The earth reacted to everything right along with me while I was growing up."

"That's singular to us impurities. Pure elementals don't have a clue what their ethos might be until after they've been evoked," Levi said. "I imagine our dual ethos leaves us brimming with power that would just spill over whenever we had an outburst of emotion."

I grimaced. "I think I may have set off an earthquake the day the police declared Eren dead."

"I set books on fire when my mother insisted I read them, and the flames spread, causing us to lose half of our ancestral home in Eldur."

"I had bees sting my twin when he wouldn't let me borrow his bike."

Levi laughed. "That sounds like it was intentional."

"Most definitely," I conceded. "So, how does it feel to get beat by me?" I asked, nodding towards the thriving plant amidst Levi's scorching flames.

"Careful. We can't have you developing a god complex," he said, a smirk playing on his lips. "But, to answer your question, it's refreshing to finally have a worthy opponent."

"Let's hope, for your sake, we stay fighting on the same side," I teased.

"For everyone's sake," he said as he stood, extending his hand out to me. "But you'll never need to worry about me."

I took his hand, but he didn't let go once I was on my feet. Instead, his hand lingered over mine, his thumb stroking my palm. It lasted only a moment before Levi let go and walked away.

I trailed behind him, holding my hand up to my chest, and I could almost sense his hand in it, still.

I FOLLOWED LEVI UNTIL WE REACHED A SMALL RIVER THAT flowed near the cabin. I heard the rough water frothing and crashing as we approached and came up with a wide range of excuses as to why I couldn't get in. I must've had a crazy look in my eye when we stopped by the banks because Levi grabbed my hand and squeezed it.

"I'm not going to ask you to get in just yet, though I will," he said. "We're here so you can practice growing in the water. It was fun to see you work through my fire, but it won't be me you'll be fighting out there—you'll be fighting the Icis."

Levi was right. I needed to get used to being around water. I needed to get over this ridiculous fear if I expected to be of any help in saving Grant. So, I nodded and took a deep breath to steady myself.

"Now, plant your feet and summon something out of the river," he instructed.

I closed my eyes, focusing my thoughts on unearthing the roots from underneath the riverbed. The earth sensed my urgency because, just like that, we heard rocks being disturbed, clattering against one another, and then a sizable root broke through the river's surface and curled upwards towards the sky.

"Alright," Levi muttered, staring at the root in astonishment. "I see you don't need any help in this department." And then he removed his shirt.

"What are you doing?" I asked him, my pulse quickening as he unbuttoned his jeans.

"We should rinse off before heading back," he said in a casual tone.

He stood in front of me now, completely nude. It took everything I had to keep my eyes from wandering below his waist, so I entertained myself with everything above it.

Levi was strong, but not excessively so, as though it were his natural state and not something he actively worked for, and his chest was bare, other than the trail that led down to . . . *oh god.*

My eyes flashed back up to his face and, though his

expression didn't change, he absolutely saw me sneak a quick look.

I could feel my cheeks burning, but I refused to look away. I mean, we were both adults here. And, frankly, I wanted to see more.

He walked into the river until the water reached his waist before turning back to me. "I understand this is difficult for you, but you need to reclaim what they took from you. Come," he said, holding out his arms. "Let's make new, positive memories with water." When I didn't respond right away, he added, "I can turn around if you'd like me to."

"No," I said. "I'd rather you didn't."

If I was to do this, I wanted him to watch. I wanted to make this anything other than what my nerves were making it out to be, so I carefully pulled my shirt over my head, fully aware that I wore nothing underneath. Levi's eyes hovered over my breasts appreciatively, far longer than a gentleman should, before locking with mine again as I slipped out of my jeans.

I stood there for a moment to ready myself, searching for the courage in his eyes. Then, slowly, I made my way into the river. The moment my feet touched the water, my breath caught in my throat, and I squeezed my eyes shut. I tried to think about anything else other than the feel of it as I walked in further, but my thoughts reverted back to the hole—to Nerio's cruel face as he poured his acid on me from above.

I jumped at the feel of hands on my waist and opened my eyes to see Levi.

He stood close. Intimately close. Close enough that I could smell his faint wood-smoke scent mingled with the clean algae smell of the river. He smelled so damn delectable that if someone were to take his scent and make a candle out of it, it would be eternally back-ordered.

Levi pulled me out of my trance and into the river. We waded through the leaves and twigs, over the slimy rocks and silt underfoot, until the shockingly warm water barely covered our chests—Levi's doing, I imagined.

"Thanks for heating it up for me," I said, hoping to break the silence and, in turn, my nerves.

He didn't say anything. Instead, his eyes pierced into mine exploringly, suggestively—in a way that made my heart stammer at wild intervals in my chest.

"Do I look like a Valterra?" I blurted out, but I meant to ask whether he liked the name. I just couldn't think straight with his eyes boring into mine.

He took a moment to consider. "It's a strong, unique name," he said, repositioning his hands until they rested on my hips. "I think it suits you perfectly, though I think that has more to do with the fact that it belongs to you rather than the name itself."

Oh, that's a good answer . . .

I bit my lip to hide my smile, and Levi's eyes flickered to them in response.

"You have got to stop looking at me like that," I laughed, attempting to suppress the fluttery sensation in my stomach.

"Why?" he asked, tightening his grip. "Maybe I'm looking at you like this for a reason."

Well, well, well . . . message received.

I arched my back to dip my hair into the water while the pull of the river's strong current kept Levi's hands clutching my waist and, instead of focusing on the anxiety this gave me, I focused on how Levi must've taken the image of me. I could feel his eyes taking in every inch as it stretched out before him, and when I emerged, his eyes were ablaze with desire.

My heart stopped, but, this time, not from my fear of the water.

"Is it your first time?" Levi asked, noticing my intake of breath.

"No," I whispered. "But I'm scared."

He eyed me questioningly for a moment before finally understanding and rested his head against my forehead. "Me too," he said. He placed his hand against my cheek, his thumb trailing over my bottom lip—as though he were asking for consent. Then, when I didn't pull away, his thumb gently parted them.

I let my tongue graze his thumb and watched his eyes burn with intensity at my invitation.

Then, slowly, to be sure I saw, he placed his thumb to his mouth and tasted me before bowing his head to meet his lips to mine.

He kissed me tenderly at first, testing our connection. He must've liked what he found because his tongue made its way into my mouth, luring mine to join his, which it was only too eager to do. Then, the softness dissipated, and the kiss intensified, taking on a life of its own.

The heat radiating off his body, his rich wood-smoke scent, and the sweet taste of his lips flooded my senses.

He drew me in closer until my breasts pressed against his chest, which only excited him further, making him grunt into my mouth. It tasted *divine* on my tongue. He formed a knot in my hair with one hand while the other felt its way down my side, lingering to give my breast a firm, sensual squeeze before continuing further downwards.

Levi's hand wrapped around my knee, lifting me up

over his length. And it was rock-hard. The heat and feel of him between my legs made me want to scream.

At that moment, I craved nothing more than for Levi to take me right then and there. I wanted him to fuck me senseless.

"Valerie?"

Our heads snapped towards the woods to see Hestia making her way over to us, and before I could even think of what to do, Levi plunged himself into the river.

I crossed my arms around my chest before Hestia turned towards the sound of the splash, cursed, and swiveled back around.

"Yer shouldn't be out here this late, lass!" Hestia yelled, more upset at finding me in a compromising position than the fact that I was out here at all.

Levi's fingers trailed up my inner thighs, and I squeezed my legs together, trapping them.

"I was just cleaning up," I said, pushing Levi's head down deeper only to see his air bubbles rise to the surface.

"Haste ye back! Don't want the lads to catch you in this state," she grumbled before stalking off.

When I could be sure she wasn't within earshot anymore, I pulled on Levi's hair, and he came with it.

"Ah!" he protested.

I nudged him hard. "You're an idiot."

He laughed. "You heard the woman. Let's get out of here before *the lads* see you," he said, winking at me.

As we giggled our way out of the river and into our clothes, it struck me just how different Levi behaved with me as opposed to the others. This man exuded passion and zeal and laughed without restraint. Nothing like the apathetic, haughty man I encountered months ago in the cave. Is this what lay in store for me, too?

"I wonder if they'd still fear you if they saw you the

way that I did," I wondered as we made our way back to the cabin.

"I choose not to show them this side of me, just like you shouldn't show them all of you," Levi said, his tone serious now. "It's that fear that keeps them at bay, Valerie. We will always be a threat to them. And by them, I mean all of them—not just the Icis. So if there's anything you learn from me, let it be that."

"Is that why you didn't accept the role of authority?"

"It was definitely a contributing factor," he said. "But mainly, if I had, the Icis would have considered me a threat and taken us out years ago. So I needed to seem indifferent to it. I guess I sort of am. I mean, I didn't ask to be born with this."

He sounded so . . . defeated, and my heart ached for him. Everything he had ever done had to be so carefully calculated to ensure his survival, and it drained me just to think about it.

I wanted to change the subject; I wanted to see him happy again. "Why appoint Nur?" I asked and felt relieved when he smiled. I'd prefer he talk about his friend.

"Aiden is a decent guy, but Nur is *kind*. He takes the time to weigh his options before settling on a decision. He was also the only one who considered saving me when . . . Well, when my life fell apart. So if I had to pretend to be beneath anyone, I would rather it be Nur."

We had gotten back to the cabin to see Hestia and George eating by the fire. They both looked puzzled as they took us in, and I mentally kicked myself for not having thought to come up with an explanation as to why Levi was also soaked. But, as luck would have it, Hestia thought one up all on her own through self-delusion.

"What did I tell you, lass? Suppose he would've wandered into yer part of the river," she scolded.

I commended Levi for his ability to keep a straight face as he picked up a peach and sat next to Hestia. I had a bit more trouble doing so. "Yes, well, fortunately, he didn't," I muttered, sitting on the remaining rock adjacent to George.

Eika emerged from the woods and sat beside me. I gave her a good scratch behind her ear as she settled by my feet.

"I don't know if I'll ever get used to that," George said. "Do I get a shadow at one point, too?"

"I've never seen someone without an animal affinity have such a strong pull on one before," Hestia said.

A stiff breeze whipped over us, rustling our campsite and making me shiver.

"You're cold?" George asked.

I nodded and decided not to object when George wrapped his arm around me. An immature part of me wanted to see Levi's reaction, and he didn't disappoint.

Levi let out a harsh breath, first glaring at the arm and then at me. Then, he brought the peach to his mouth and took a deliberately carnal bite out of it.

I had to cross my legs to control what it did to me, but I was over my little game in an instant, embarrassed to have played it at all. I wanted to be alone with Levi, and I wanted him to know it.

"I'm exhausted, actually. I think I'll just head in for the night," I announced.

Though I didn't bother looking at George, I could sense the disappointment wafting off of him.

"Good idea, lassie," Hestia said. "There's work to be done tomorrow. Sleep well."

I shot one last glance at Levi before marching into the cabin. I only knew he followed me when the door took a moment longer to close behind me.

"Don't do that."

I turned to see Levi glowering at me. "Do what?"

He wasn't fooled by my response. "Don't act coy, Valerie," he replied, his tone harsh. "You're trying to elicit a response from me, and it's beneath you."

I sprawled out on one of the mattresses set against the wall and stared at the ceiling.

"Do I have to say why?" he asked, his voice booming.

"No," I sighed. I knew why and I didn't care to hear it said aloud. I could feel my eyes tearing up, so I covered my face with both hands to hide them should they spill.

Someone opened the door and, though I didn't lift my hands to see, I figured who it was. Levi hadn't exactly been whispering.

"Everything okay in here?" I heard George ask. "Did I miss something?"

"No," Levi spat. "Valerie and I talk all the time when you're not around. Look, I'll show you." And then the door slammed in what I imagined was George's face. "*Fuck*," Levi cursed as something crashed against the floor.

I uncovered my face to see a stack of Hestia's botany books scattered all over the ground.

When Levi saw my expression, he rushed to sit beside me. "Did I scare you?"

"No."

"You're crying."

I wiped my eyes with the palms of my hands. "I'm fine. I just . . . I'm fine."

He wiped away a rogue tear. "Talk to me," he whispered.

"Why does everything have to be so hard?" I asked, breaking before I even finished the question.

My head swarmed with everything that had ever gone wrong in my life, now adding that I would forever need to sleep with one eye open for my sake and for Levi's. We were barely getting by convincing them that we should exist at all, let alone together, and the idea of having to suppress our feelings, however new they were, devastated me.

Levi watched me, his brows drawn together. "I shouldn't have kissed you, Valerie. I'm sorry."

I rolled my eyes at him. "Oh, please. As if you could've prevented this," I said, waving my hand between us to lighten the mood and attempted a smile. After all, Levi's been white-knuckling his whole life, while this was only my first brush with my new reality.

"Things will be different for you," he said, tucking a lock of hair behind my ear. "I'll make sure of it."

"No," I said. "I'm the one who showed up out of thin air, making everything more difficult for you than it had to be." I didn't know how, but I was determined to make this work. "Let me worry about that."

I walked over to pick up Hestia's books from the floor when I noticed an outline on the planks. "What is this?" I whispered, tracing it with my fingers.

Levi came up from behind me and tapped on the planks with the heel of his shoe. The sound echoed as though it were hollow underneath. "This leads some-where," he said.

Levi pried off the planks to reveal a steel hatch that had been hidden beneath our feet this entire time.

I knelt beside him as he attempted to open it, but it was sealed shut. "A bunker?"

"Hestia's a thorough woman," Levi muttered.

The following day, Hestia had me train with George, who could summon earthquakes, though he couldn't do so on a large scale—yet. Combining my creation with his destructive abilities made it a fun challenge since we both had to work despite the other.

That is until I found a way to counteract him.

As the earth fractured underneath us, I had my roots spread in a web-like formation, securing themselves too far underground for his ethos to reach before charging to my aid. I found it only too easy to work around him then, but I couldn't let it show, so while I naturally won some battles, I feigned to lose others.

Levi cheered during those I chose to win, much to George's chagrin. And after the fights I elected to lose, he'd wink to show he knew better. Though I still wished I could use full force, it was *exhilarating*.

At one point, as I ran across the branches of a cotton-wood, I saw Eika making her way through the trees on my right. She attempted to keep up with me, but there was a gap between the branches ahead of her. Before I could panic, she locked eyes with me and used a different path, avoiding the gap that would have undoubtedly caused her to fall.

"Am I crazy, or did she just read my thoughts?" I asked Hestia as I guided my bark to lower me towards the others. Eika met up with me, rubbing her head against my legs.

"The two of ya have formed a special bond," Hestia said, watching her with a smile. "Yer been claimed, so I reckon yer might need to take her with ya when yer go. A more loyal companion yer won't find."

I beamed at her, thrilled at the idea that I wouldn't have to go through life alone. "And when do you think that'll be? I mean, when will I be ready to go?"

"There's no denyin' yer have a natural knack for it, not much else I could teach ya," Hestia said. "Yer don't need me anymore."

Hestia looked to Levi, who nodded in agreement. And, when Hestia turned back to me, her eyes were glossy, almost as though she were proud of me.

WE MADE OUR WAY BACK TO THE CABIN TO PACK BUT decided to have lunch together one final time. I sat with Hestia, listening to her parting wisdom while Levi cut up fruit for us.

I watched strands of Levi's jet-black hair fall over his eyes as he cut the bananas into perfect bite-sized pieces—quite the perfectionist—admiring the way his eyebrows knit together when he concentrated on something.

Levi must've sensed me watching him because he looked up, and when I was sure the others weren't looking, I mouthed "adorable" at him.

Levi's answering smile, the way it made the corner of his eyes and nose crinkle, sent my heart soaring, but the effect he had on me was equal parts exhilarating as it was alarming. I wished I could embrace the new feelings he stirred within me, but the tiny sensible part of my brain urged me to pump the brakes, and I looked away.

Hestia brought my attention back to her, saying she'd care for Eika until I returned since the lake would be too much for the panther to bear, and though I understood, I was still saddened to hear it. I had no idea when or if I'd be able to come back, and the thought of Eika possibly forgetting about me made my stomach clench.

When I mentioned this to Hestia, she asked, "Will *you* forget about Eika?"

"Of course not."

"Then I don't see why yer troubling yerself with such talk when the bond goes both ways, lass."

"You're right," I said, but my concern was still very much real, and it must've shown on my face because Hestia gave me a knowing side-eye. But she dropped the subject, asking instead whether I felt comfortable managing my ethos after her training.

"It's hard to say, seeing as I'm really early in my Natura career, or really late if this ends poorly," I told her. "But I'm as ready as I'll ever be."

"Wait. You're not fighting, are you?" George asked in disbelief.

"I am," I said, trying not to get too offended by his tone.

He stared at me for a moment, waiting for me to tell him I was joking, but I only stared back. "But, Valerie... you wouldn't help. You'd only get in the way."

"George!" Hestia protested.

"What? She's trained for a couple months, and now she thinks she could fight against the Icis who have dedicated their entire lives to this?"

Hestia and Levi were taken aback, but what surprised me most was my lack of rebuttal.

"You're assuming she shares your personal limitations," Levi said, his tone thick with contempt. "You forget she's a different species. None of you are anywhere near her caliber. No offense, Hestia," he added as an afterthought.

"None taken," Hestia muttered, though her expression said otherwise. "Yer not wrong."

Even if George raised his concerns out of fondness for me, I still didn't appreciate how he chose to do so, and I regretted allowing him to win all those times before.

"Let's go, Valerie," Levi said. "I know Fintan, and we're making him restless the longer we stay out here. The man isn't known for his patience."

I shot George a sullen glance before making my way to

where Levi stood. "Nothing I've learned of Fintan, I've learned consensually," I muttered, lowering my head on impulse.

I was hurt. Even though I had consciously chosen to only portray my full abilities to Levi, it still stung to hear George question me. I mean, what if he was right? How could a month of training, even if around-the-clock, be enough to surmount a lifetime's worth?

"Fintan's a prick, but he's got salt in the game," Levi replied, seemingly unaware of my mood, but then he gave my hand a tight squeeze. "George doesn't know what he's talking about," he whispered.

I nodded to show I heard him, even though I didn't quite believe him.

Hestia walked over to us, clearing her throat before facing me. "My bonnie lass," she said, "there will be a myriad of occasions where yer will be inclined to question yerself. But, you must never allow yer emotions to influence yer power. It's unpredictable when you must be calculatin'," she said, pausing to let the words settle. "Have faith in yer ethos, Valerie. Trust that it will never betray you."

And just like that, Hestia's rousing words dispelled every ounce of doubt George had instilled in me.

CHAPTER TWELVE
HISS HISS

EREN

I COULD HEAR A PIN DROP FROM A MILE AWAY. THE cacophony of sounds made it difficult to focus, so I resorted to isolating the sounds by distance in my mind—a laboring effort.

I couldn't have imagined this being my ethos. I had no clue air had so much to do with one's sense of hearing. Even though a part of me wished I had obtained a combat ethos, I couldn't ignore the obvious calling. Here I was, being asked to keep tabs on the happenings of our enemies, and fate granted me with a heightened sense of hearing. If that wasn't a sign that I was destined for this work, then I didn't know what was.

After Calder received my message of Valerie's evocation, he insisted I be evoked as well. Only after threatening to end me and just about every other person in the room if we didn't get our shit together. The Ignis had been almost as angry to hear the news as the Icis were. Almost.

Seraphina was livid. Shouting profanities at Levi for having been so rash in making the decision. A decision that Nur reminded him wasn't his to make.

Levi watched them stone-faced. A feat in and of itself with an angry demon that could literally turn herself into fire barking at him. "Would you like to pick up this conversation some other time?" he asked Seraphina. "I'm worried about your temper."

But, of course, this only upset her further.

"My temper is fine," she hissed. "I'm actually just warming up."

"That's what concerns me."

"Did you expect us to thank you?"

"Actually, I did," he said. "Fate dropped a game-changer on your lap, and you all would have squandered it had it not been for me."

He was right. Though the Ignis distrusted Levi to some degree, they appreciated that his existence kept the Icis from finishing what they had started years ago. But that didn't mean they liked it. On the contrary, their fear would never have swayed them to enable another impurity. That was the one thing the Ignis and Icis could agree on.

The day Levi and Valerie returned, I got the feeling something may have happened between them while they were off in the Origin. They seemed too comfortable around each other, almost chummy, and that would certainly complicate things.

Since I had yet to be evoked, I needed to investigate through more traditional methods. So, I walked into the infirmary to check if Valerie had written anything down in her boredom only to find Levi posted against the wall, and I stopped in my tracks at the sight of him.

"What are you up to?" he asked, articulating each word deliberately. The question was simple enough, but there was most definitely an edge to it.

I swallowed my nerves, wishing I only imagined it. "Looking for my sister," I replied, rubbing my forehead with my fingertips, afraid I looked as suspicious as I felt. "How about you?"

"Same," he said. Nothing more, yet his eyes remained fixed on me. Why was he not saying more?

"Okay," I said, praying that I was only projecting. "Val's not here, so I'll be on my way then." Though the tension in the room was palpable, Levi's expression didn't change, but his eerie silence frightened me more than if he would've outed me on the spot.

I struggled to keep my composure as I left the room, but I was sweating like a pig in a slaughterhouse.

I couldn't live like this. We needed to act *now*.

As soon as I was evoked, I was brought to Calder. He seethed in his office, throwing ice shards turned to steel against the wall. I winced at the grating sound, which otherwise wouldn't have pained me had it not been for my newly amplified sense.

"I expect you to become a useful part of this endeavor now, Eren," Calder said. "We have done our part. You are evoked and, now that fate has granted you this ethos, there should be no more surprises. No more excuses."

"When, if I may ask, will we act? I'm on thin ice with

the Ignis. I'm surrounded by those demons day in and day out, and I could swear Levi has been looking at me funny."

"What?" Calder asked, turning to me abruptly. "Does he know?"

"I can't be sure, but I have a feeling he might. We need to do something before he puts two and two together, or I'm dead. What are we waiting for?" I hoped to stay calm and collected, but my desperation seeped through the more I spoke.

"I will not speak tactics with a *Ventus*," Calder spat, throwing another steel icicle hurling towards the wall. "You're right to be afraid, but don't forget your part in this. You took your eyes off your sister, and now she's been evoked—forcing us to take down two impurities as opposed to one. We had to rework the entire plan in light of your negligence," he said but took a moment to collect himself —realizing that his words only increased my anxiety. "Just, calm down. As you said, if he knew, then you'd be dead, and you're not. The sooner you give us something that might actually benefit us, the sooner we can act," he said, waving his hand to signal Salil and Laec to escort me out.

"Yes, sir," I replied. There wasn't much else for me to say. Instead of gathering information to help the cause, I had become the bearer of bad news. And Calder had no qualms with shooting the messenger.

"By God, man. Get a grip," Salil said under his breath as he ushered me out.

"Easy for you to say from the safety of your castle," I muttered.

"We won't be safe for long," Laec said. "Don't forget, it's us who will be fighting on the field."

That shut me up. We all had a role to play in this war, and I knew that my time had finally come to shift the tide to our advantage.

I would not let Calder down again. My life, and Grant's, depended on it.

Chapter Thirteen

Red Rag to a Bull

VALERIE

"I can't talk to you if you're committed to misunderstanding me," Levi said.

We were huddled in Nur's office, listening to the lecture of a lifetime. Levi argued back and forth about my release, but the others weren't any closer to appreciating what it meant for us.

Nur fumed quietly in his chair. The bulk of the arguments stemmed from Seraphina and Aiden, who stood on either side of him. Fintan hung back, staring daggers at me since they knew nothing of his involvement—though, he looked at me that way before as well, so perhaps it wasn't part of his act.

Levi sat across from them, his expression unflappable, with me at his side. I crossed my arms and tried to keep my mouth shut. Nothing I said could change their minds. A single word out of my mouth would only remind them of my existence—an existence they would gladly terminate if they could.

"Nur," Levi said, pointing his words at the only person whose opinion mattered to him. "The Icis have had years to work out a way to counteract me. But, having Valerie on our side, evoked, gives us the edge we need. Since they won't have time to formulate a new plan, we'll have the advantage. We'll finally have a shot against them. All I'm asking you to do is think about it."

Nur watched Levi, his fingers laced together, trying to discern what to do. Finally, after a long pause, he said, "What's done is done. And, seeing as I can't undo what you did, we might as well use her, but promise me one thing."

Aiden began to object, but Nur waved him away.

"If ever a moment arises where she becomes a danger to us," Nur continued, "I need you to promise me that you'll take care of it. Valerie will be your responsibility."

"Take care of it?" I repeated, sitting up in my chair.

They regarded each other in silence, neither choosing to elaborate.

The drastic shift in his opinion of me left me floored. I couldn't believe this was coming from Nur when he had been so kind and gentle with me in the past. And his bold choice to ask this of Levi in my presence didn't slip my notice either. It was a power move, Nur's way of putting me in my place, and I took note.

I would do anything to know what went on in Levi's head, but I didn't have to wonder for long.

"I promise," was all he said, an inscrutable look on his face, and I lowered my head instinctively as the two words tore an unexpected hole through my chest.

I mean, Levi didn't specify how he'd carry out said "promise." Still, even so, it was an unnecessary addition to an already towering list of reasons why Levi might think the idea of us together was too much trouble to even consider.

Nur watched him for a moment longer before nodding —satisfied with Levi's response. "Now, if you'll excuse me," he said, standing up, "I have other matters to attend to."

Levi and I remained seated as the room cleared, and I jumped like a cat on a hot tin roof when Seraphina slammed the door behind her.

"This was expected," Levi said, not looking at me.

I kept my eyes glued to Nur's chair, too. "I was almost sure the fruit we brought back for them would've softened the blow."

He didn't react to my attempt at a joke. The promise he made lingered in the air, creating a menacing rift between us that was nearly visible.

I only hoped it wasn't impenetrable.

LATER THAT DAY, I MET UP WITH CORA AND HER SISTERS, who led me to what they called the "observance" room. Iri and Fiametta ran off to socialize with the other children while I stood in shock as I heard exactly what we would be observing.

Cora explained only one individual could acquire a particular ethos at any given time as they were exclusive. So, when a person grew too old to utilize their ethos efficiently, the ethos had to be "recovered" into a new host, and, as it happened, Seraphina's grandmother, Eilidh, had reached that condition.

"Can't she get better?" I asked.

"She's not wine," Cora said. "She won't get better with age."

Zoran joined us as a crowd formed around the woman.

"Sorry, I'm late, ladies. Did I miss the blessed event?" he asked, only to notice my horrified expression. "It's the circle of life, Valerie. Her ethos is too powerful, and we'll already be without it for the foreseeable future. There's no telling when it'll cycle back."

"How old is too old?" I asked Cora. The woman didn't look a day over sixty.

"You'd have to cut her open and count the rings," Zoran muttered.

Cora nudged him, laughing. "I think she's over two hundred, but I'm not too sure."

I gaped at her, but before I could confirm whether it was a joke, Fintan approached us.

"I'm excited to see how well you work as fodder on the field," Fintan said to me, sneering.

"Did you really come all this way just to say that?" Zoran asked, squaring up to him.

"It's fine, Zoran," I said. "Let's not dignify that with a response."

Fintan gave a quick, disgusted snort, turning away from us as though we weren't worth his time, and sparked a conversation with a burly man with elegant braids to his left instead.

"I hope he has a horrible day," Zoran muttered.

I shrugged, finding it easier to ignore Fintan's catty behavior rather than give him the satisfaction of engaging. "Anyway, this is kind of a weird time to give you this," I said to Cora, digging into my pocket. "But, before I forget, I brought you something from the Origin. It's nothing crazy, just something I thought you might like," I added, pulling out her gift.

Cora's eyes lit up—something I didn't think possible with a set of voids for eyes. "You got me a present?" she squealed, weighing it in her hand. "It's so light."

"Must be her hopes and dreams for you," Zoran quipped.

"Oh no," I said. "I discarded those a while ago."

Cora laughed at our banter as she unwrapped the receipt from the gas station, only to gasp as she raised the tiny magic eight ball in her hand. "How cute! I love miniature versions of things," she gushed, aggressively shaking it.

"Then you'd just love what Fintan has to show you," Zoran said, knowing full well that Fintan was within earshot.

Fintan scowled as we laughed at his expense. "Why do you pick battles you can't win, Zoran? So desperate for another black eye, are you?"

"Why?" I asked, positioning myself between them. "Are you gonna give it to him? No one is afraid of you, Fintan."

He took a step in my direction only to stop, remembering I had been evoked. "I don't recall asking the fairy," he said, instead.

Cora scoffed. "Was that supposed to be an insult? Try harder."

"Eat shit, Cora," he spat.

The man with the braids turned back to us in disapproval. "Shh! The ceremony is about to start. Show some respect."

"Sorry, Kai," Cora muttered.

We all sunk back to the scolding just as Nur approached the older woman in the center of the room. I stood on the tips of my toes to get a better look, only to be disappointed when I didn't find Levi in the crowd.

Eren walked over to us, and I pulled him in, tucking him under my arm, but he was tense. Probably just as nervous as I was about the ceremony.

And then, all conversations came to a halt. Nur

reached out to the older woman, who must've been Eilidh, and held her hands in his. He smiled at her, and she smiled softly back. Then, he began to speak in a language I didn't understand, though I recognized it as the same language spoken by Hestia during my evocation.

I could see Seraphina on the other side, her expression somber, as tears streamed down her face. It was the first time I had been able to sympathize with her. The first time I had ever seen a genuine softness in her countenance. I wondered if I could ever standby and watch my loved one be executed for the sake of a single power.

No, I could never.

Ren wormed her way through the crowd to stand beside Seraphina. She rested her hand ever so gently on Seraphina's wrist as she whispered something in her ear. And then, Seraphina turned to her and placed her lips against Rens.

But, before I could process their kiss, Nur let go of Eilidh and stepped back. He lifted his hands, and a gust of fiery wind spun between them. Then, with a swift wave of his hands, the fire vortex traveled away from him and towards Eilidh, growing larger and larger until it fully engulfed the old woman.

I slapped my hands over my mouth to keep from crying out as Eilidh thrashed on the ground where she had fallen. Surprisingly, she didn't scream, but it only made the sight that much more disturbing.

Eren watched with wide eyes, visibly shaken, the only other person in the room reacting like one would expect, while the Ignis merely hung their heads in silence. No one spoke as the fire consumed her unresponsive body, filling the room with smoke and the smell of burning flesh, but it was more than I could bear.

I ran out of the room to escape the smoke and stench,

but not quick enough, as my breakfast made its way back up and onto the cave floor.

CORA FOUND ME IN THE INFIRMARY MOMENTS LATER. Though she saw my reaction to their ceremony, she didn't comment on it. Instead, she sat beside me.

"I think it's about that time, Valerie," she said.

"Huh?"

"I've come to collect. To cash in the favor," she clarified.

I drew in a long breath. "I figured you would have changed your mind by now."

"Changed my mind? I've been preparing for this my entire life, much to the amusement of everybody here," she said. "But, they need me now more than ever, now that we're down an ethos."

"You told me your ethos isn't meant for combat."

"That doesn't mean I can't fight in other ways. I've trained with Kai and Vesta since I was nine, Valerie. I'm ready to fight the Icis alongside my sisters and my people," she said, fussing with the silver chain on her wrist. "I don't expect you to understand."

"I have two brothers, Cora," I snapped. "One of which is being held prisoner by them."

"So you'll do it? You'll talk to Nur for me?"

I massaged the back of my neck as I contemplated her request. No matter what I said, Cora would find a way to fight. With or without my help. But if I were to support her, then I could devise a way to protect Cora from herself.

"Fine," I muttered. "I'll talk to Nur."

Cora beamed at me and went on to hint in a not-so-subtle way that perhaps I would like to bathe. I agreed, but only because I hoped to run into Levi later on. So, she escorted me to the bathing room, cleared it by announcing my arrival, and took her place against the wall to give me privacy.

Once I gathered my supplies, I took a deep breath and walked up to the quiet river. I slowly placed my right foot into the water and left it there until my rising panic subsided. I reminded myself that I was not in pain at that moment and that any pain I registered was but a remnant of the pain I had felt in the past. Then, I placed my other foot in and repeated the process.

Gradually, I made my way inside until I was chest-deep. Though my heart raced, my will was strong. I dipped my head in and came up laughing.

I was in the river—like, actually *inside* of it.

I washed as profusely as I could, taking advantage of my semi-calm mind since I didn't know how long it would last until finally, I was the cleanest I had been in months. I sat before the singular mirror leaning against the stone wall and decided to take some time to primp myself.

I separated each potential curl and twirled them so they'd dry in place and rubbed a bit of red rouge I found lying around on my cheeks and lips, hoping whoever it belonged to wouldn't mind. The lighting here was dim, but I was satisfied with what I could see. This was the closest to my old self I would ever get while in a cave within a different dimension.

As I made my way to the exit with a freeing sense of accomplishment, I heard the tail end of a conversation Cora was having with someone.

"It's been hard after what Nerio put her through," she said. "But it's helped that we have Ren to hydrate her. I just give her time to sort herself out."

I rounded the corner to see Eren standing by Cora.

"What did you do in there? You look great!" Cora exclaimed, reaching out to feel my hair.

"I just bathed," I muttered, swatting her hand away.

"You do look nice," Eren agreed, though his tone was laced with concern. "How do you feel?"

I frowned at Cora and looked back at him with a tight smile. "I'm good, thanks. I was just taking a bath. It's no big deal."

"Did you do something to your hair?" she asked.

"This is how I always look, Cora."

"She was just telling me——" Eren began.

"I heard, and she's exaggerating. I'm perfectly fine."

They regarded each other briefly before Cora read the room and excused herself.

"I'm your brother, Val. I don't know why you feel you can't talk to me."

"There's nothing to talk about," I said. "I'm fine. And I don't appreciate Cora implying otherwise and making you worry."

Eren raised an eyebrow but shrugged. "If you say so."

"I do," I said, bumping shoulders with him to lighten the mood. "Now, I know your birthday isn't for a couple of months, but with everything going on, I just wanted to get you a little something just for the hell of it." I placed the second magic eight ball and a pack of Eren's favorite candy, Airheads, into his palm.

Eren regarded them with a blank expression.

"It's not much, I know, but I didn't know how long it would be before I saw you, so I had to pick something with a more forgiving expiration date."

Still, nothing.

I tugged uneasily at my earlobe, grasping now how stupid the random gifts appeared. "So, how about we hang out tonight?" I offered in their stead. "We could play cards or get Cora and Zoran to join us for a game of charades? It's weird. We've barely seen each other since we've been here. I can never find you."

"Weird would be to play games while the Icis have Grant."

I shrunk back, shocked at the edge in his tone. And, though I knew it was unwarranted, guilt washed over me. "There's nothing we could do about that right now, Eren," I said as calmly as I could. "Levi and Nur said that he's most likely fine since he's a pure Ventus, like you. Either way, we're getting him out of there soon."

His ears perked up at that. "How soon? Did Nur tell you when?"

"Well, no, but before the end of the week, I imagine. Nothing's stopping Nur, now that I've been evoked since Levi's sure my spooky druid-ish powers will be enough to even the playing field," I said, wiggling my fingers at him spiritedly.

He didn't laugh. "You go on ahead and chill with Cora. I can't go tonight. I promised Kai I'd help him build a bed for his kid who's grown out of his crib."

"You? Building a bed? How much help can that be?" I teased.

"Enough, apparently," he snapped.

"Are you mad at me or something?" I asked, fed up with his attitude.

He sighed, though he didn't look me in the eye. "No, there's just a lot going on. Thanks for this," he said, cramming the gifts into his pocket. "But, I have to go. Otherwise, Kai's son will have to squeeze into the crib again tonight." He proceeded to give me an awkward hug before turning to go.

Eren was undoubtedly upset with me, though about what? I had no idea. I stood there for a while, racking my brain for what I could've possibly done to set him off, but, for the life of me, nothing came to mind. So, I figured I'd let him cool off and come to me when he was ready to talk.

As I tidied up the mess I had made in the infirmary, arms encircled me from behind. I spun around, and I could swear my heart skipped a beat when I saw Levi's face only inches away from mine. He sported a smile so big, so wholesome that it crinkled his eyes and nose. And, it was quite simply the cutest thing I had ever seen.

"Well, hello there," I said, wrapping my arms around him in return.

"You look incredible," he said, nestling his face into my neck, which in turn made me shiver.

I smiled, knowing it was his way of congratulating me on my successful run-in with water. "Why, thank you. And to what do I owe this pleasure?"

He reached behind him and pointed at two bundles he had placed on the tray. "I thought we could have dinner together. If you don't already have plans, that is. I bet a stunning woman like yourself must already be spoken for on such short notice."

I blushed like an innocent little schoolgirl. "You're in luck. I deemed my other potential suitor for tonight quite unworthy."

"That poor bastard," he said, stepping back and dividing the food for us. "But, his loss is my gain." He took one last thing out of the brown bag and placed it behind his back as we prepared to eat. "I have a surprise for you."

I bounced on the cot in excitement. "What is it?"

He swung his arm back, and a perfectly round peach

rested in his hand. "I saved you the last one so you could have it for dessert."

I placed my hand over my chest, honored at having been thought of. "We'll share it."

"No, no. I saved it for you."

It turned out we were both hungrier than we thought, so we ate in relative silence, but not the awkward kind. It was peaceful. Natural. Neither of us felt the need to fill the conversational lulls.

Once I had my fill of the main course, I dove into the peach. We had picked out the less than ripe ones back at the cabin so that they'd last a while here, and so the peach was plump and juicy.

"Maybe I will have some," Levi decided, and before I could say anything, he met his lips to mine. He kissed me softly, only to part my lips with his tongue and scoop up some of the fruit.

My heart stopped. I watched Levi in awe as he savored the peach he had just taken from my mouth as though it were the most ordinary thing in the world.

Holy shit. Why was that one of the hottest things to ever happen to me?

I couldn't explain why the action, and the fact that he seemed totally relaxed about it, made me feel tingly below the waist. But I liked it—*a lot.*

"So, what have you been up to today?" he asked me. He kept the nonchalant look on his face, but I could see an intensity in his eyes, proving he wasn't as unfazed as he would've liked me to believe.

"I watched the ceremony," I said, raising my brows to hint at how I felt about it.

"It must've seemed drastic to you, I imagine."

"You could say that. Though I knew nothing of this

world until a few months, so who am I to judge? I also noticed you weren't there," I added after a short pause.

"I'm not purely Ignis. I didn't want to intrude."

When he didn't elaborate, I wondered if he did so of his own accord or if they had asked him not to participate. It would be hypocritical to expect him to risk his life to defend them and yet exclude him from the inner workings of their community.

"Well, Ren was there. And she was more than welcomed by Seraphina," I said, waiting to see his reaction.

"Yes, because she and Seraphina are together," he said matter-of-factly.

I lowered the peach onto my lap, piercing its skin with my nail to distract myself from the dreadful envy that found its way into my heart. "I don't understand," I whispered. "How come Seraphina and Ren can make their union public while you and I are forced to hide ours in the dark recesses of the cave?"

Levi reached for my hand, stroking it with his thumb. "They can't reproduce, Valerie. But just because the Ignis aren't calling for their separation doesn't mean their union is celebrated."

I wanted to say that we could promise to never have children ourselves but felt it way too soon to mention children when our relationship had only just blossomed, so I changed the subject instead.

"Eren was acting really weird today," I said as my earlier conversation with him crept into my mind.

"How so?"

"I don't know, but he's been a total wet blanket lately. I think he's upset about something I said or did, but he ran off to help Kai without telling me why."

Levi's eyes narrowed, and he lowered his cup onto the

tray. "Are you sure that's what he said? Because Kai's off with the group gathering supplies in the Origin."

"Positive. I know Eren said Kai because it reminded me of the ceremony where Kai basically told us to shut up."

"I must've heard wrong then," he said. "I'm sure it's nothing. He's probably just on edge, so I wouldn't worry too much about it."

"That's what he told me," I agreed and then shrugged. "I just miss him, that's all."

I had spent too much time cozying up with the new people in my life and left Eren in the dust again. Why did I keep doing this? When will I learn?

CHAPTER FOURTEEN

WHITE ELEPHANT

EREN

"They're planning to act before the week is out."

Calder smiled, but it looked wildly out of place on his face. "Good. That still leaves us with a few days to work out the kinks. Is that all?"

I fiddled with my hands, wondering if I should say more.

He picked up on my hesitation and sighed. "I told her I didn't think you were strong enough. She said you had reservations but that I was wrong. Now I see that I wasn't."

My head snapped in his direction. "You *are* wrong."

"Prove it."

But, if I did, there would be no coming back from this. A line would be drawn that I would never be able to erase —years of love and comradery out the window in a single breath.

"I think you better let Grant go first," I said. "I don't understand why you still won't let me see him. I need to see him." I had meant for my request to sound absolute, but confidence was a difficult thing to hold on to with Calder's eyes on you. Calder would see through any facade I put on, having written the playbook on the concept himself.

"Let him go?" he repeated, cocking his head to the side. "Let him go where, Eren? Are you asking me to send him along with you to the Ignis compound? What point is there to a family reunion when they'll all be dead in a week?"

"I just don't see the harm in letting me see him," I said. I knew it didn't make sense, but why did I feel as though Grant wasn't safe with them here? "I mean, we're on the same side, after all."

"You talk with all the fervor of a new convert, but if you were, then I wouldn't have to pry information out of you like pulling teeth. No," Calder said, raising his hands in the air. "Apparently, you need to be motivated, Eren. So, your brother's fate is directly linked to ours. Ensure our win, and you'll ensure his."

This was why Grant wasn't safe here. Of course, Calder didn't see me as his equal. I didn't think he saw anyone that way. But Calder also didn't respect me. He didn't feel like he owed me a dime, even though I had done a great deal for him.

"Are you going to do this, Eren?" Calder asked impatiently. "Are you on the right side of this war?"

Ultimately, I had no choice. I crossed the line when I agreed to run to the Ignis as an "escaped" prisoner, and now the Ignis would never trust me again if they learned the truth. So I was forced to place all my bets on the Icis, despite the potential consequences.

I looked at him in defeat. "Before I say more, I need. . . assurances that Valerie won't be made to suffer."

Calder, without hesitation, said, "You have my word."

"Send Nerio after her, and she won't be able to function."

He slammed his fist on the table. "Atta boy."

As usual, Laec and Salil waited to escort me out, but I wasn't ready to leave just yet.

"Can I visit the church?" I asked them.

Laec studied me shrewdly but shrugged. "I guess."

"Why do you pray to him?" Salil asked, scratching the hideous scar on his throat. "It's not like he's your god."

"He may not be mine, but he *is* a god," I muttered.

Salil gave me a side-eye, but he took the bait.

Once there, they motioned for me to enter while they waited by the entrance—just as I knew they would. In this place of worship and tranquility, it was customary to enter only when you planned to pray—and nothing more.

The sanctuary, a remarkable work of functional art, spanned the entire width of the building in an impressive manner. With engraved high ceilings reinforced by ice columns, which led to a massive ice sculpture of Nereus, god of the sea, one couldn't help but feel . . . insignificant.

Icis were scattered around the grandiose room with their knees to the floor and their heads bowed. Though it was absolutely breathtaking, sightseeing was not what I had come to do.

I looked over my shoulder to ensure Salil and Laec weren't watching and hurried towards the wall. I kept close to the fringe, treading quietly, so I didn't disturb the praying Icis' until I made it towards the second exit at the far end of the church. I focused on walking with purpose as opposed to urgency. I couldn't draw more attention to myself than usual. I weaved through the halls, keeping my face down until I made it to Calder's headquarters.

I drew in a long breath before peering over the edge of the frame and let it out in a whoosh when I didn't see Calder inside.

I had to act quick. I ran over to Calder's desk, rummaging through the paperwork, aiming to find some clue as to Grant's whereabouts or anything regarding their plans for the attack. I flipped through lists of wages, special requests, and building plans. Nothing that could be of any use to me.

I cursed under my breath. There had to be something.

I glanced over a metal box Calder kept on the corner of his desk. I figured it may hold more valuable documents, so I carefully lifted the lid only to drop it when I realized what I had just seen. I froze at the sound of the cover crashing down. Then, when no one came, I opened the top again.

Inside the box was a tuft of jet-black hair and teeth—*children's teeth*.

I shut the box and exhaled slowly, trying desperately to calm my nerves. I checked to ensure I left everything how I had found it before rushing out of the office and back to the church.

The temperature had reached below freezing, but I still had to wipe away the beads of sweat rolling down my forehead. I stood against the wall as I waited for my hands to stop shaking, and I shut my eyes, struggling to ward off the image of Calder taking his trophies from the Ignis children he killed.

The man was far more heartless, far more ruthless than I had ever imagined . . . What had I done?

As I weaved through the waves of blue-haired Icis on my way back to the church, I noticed a bobbing white head that stuck out like a sore thumb in the crowd. I pushed forward to get a closer look, but it disappeared into one of their heavily guarded buildings.

"Hey!" someone called out. It was Salil. "What in the world are you doing over here?"

"I . . . I got lost," I said.

"Come," Laec ordered. "This area is only for the Icis."

"Then why did I just see a Ventus walk into that building?" I asked, my eyes fixed on it.

Laec laughed. "I highly doubt that, Eren. You must be seeing things."

"Is the stress getting to you?" Salil asked, pinching my cheek.

I swatted his hand away. "Don't touch me."

"Let's go before Calder finds out you were out of bounds," Laec said, and they ushered me out of Reota.

MY HEAD REELED BY THE TIME I RETURNED TO THE IGNIS cave. I reminded myself over and over that I had done the right thing. And yet, I couldn't shake the feeling that I had made a terrible mistake.

As I walked through the halls, it dawned on me that it was oddly peaceful. I could hear a buzz coming from deeper in the cave with my heightened sense, but there were no children running through the halls or any meandering Ignis, for that matter. I peered into the infirmary to check on Valerie, listening closely to avoid another run-in with Levi, but it was dead silent and, when I looked, she wasn't there. I turned and continued down each path, checking every room. They were all empty.

Finally, I veered back and beelined to the common room. Though I was still too far for any regular person to hear, I caught a rumble of voices, hinting that I was going in the right direction.

When I reached the hub, I could hardly take a single step inside with the Ignis crammed into the room like sardines in a can. I couldn't see past the backs of the Ignis standing at the entrance, so I excused myself and pushed through as far as I could until I reached a bubble in the crowd where Valerie and her new friends stood.

Cora, Zoran, Iri, Fiametta, and Ren stood with her, and I *hated* it. It shocked me just how much I hated it. Valerie was an impurity that shouldn't exist, and yet, here they stood, yakking it up with her as though it were the most natural thing in the world.

How did she still manage to make me feel like an outsider when it was quite literally the other way around? How could she attract so many to her while simultaneously shattering the very fabric of their beliefs?

At least the others gave her a wide berth. Not fully trusting her—as was right.

She turned in my direction when she sensed me and smiled, pulling me into their group. I struggled not to tense at her touch.

"What's going on?" I asked, careful to keep my voice neutral.

"Nur summoned us all here. We're not sure what for, yet," she said and, though she claimed not to know why, her face was lit with excitement.

I wished I could share her enthusiasm. But if she felt this was good news for them, then it was terrible news for me.

At that moment, Nur stepped onto a bench and then onto a dining table, so he towered over us. I lifted my heels to see above the sea of black hair ahead of me, searching for him.

And there he was. Levi stood right behind Nur, scanning the crowd until his eyes rested on mine, and I dropped back onto my heels, hiding behind the heads of the Ignis – the hairs on my arms rising.

I replayed that moment again and again in my mind, trying to discover anything amiss in his microexpressions like a twitch of his brow or a tightening in his jaw. Anything that could hint at what was going on inside of his head. But his face didn't divulge a thing.

I prayed this was all just a bad case of paranoia, the same way I imagined seeing the bobbing white head in Reota, but something deep within me insisted otherwise.

Nur interrupted my mental collapse to quiet the crowd, and a hush drew across the room.

"It's been almost two decades since our kind has been free to roam outside this cave. Over half of you have not set foot outside of it your entire lives. But that ends tonight. The years we've dedicated to preparing and training will now be put to the test. Our time in hiding is over, and the time to regain what has been taken from us has begun."

"My people," Nur continued, his voice mounting with intensity, "it appears the Icis have forgotten that Vulcan's blood runs through our veins, so let us remind them of what it can do. Remind them that our fires cannot be extinguished, that our fires will never relent!" he roared.

The crowd around me thundered in agreement, thrusting their fists into the air.

Nur waited for the crowd to settle. "We will pack only what is necessary to take with us to the Origin, where we will prove to the Icis what the Ignis are truly made of. So, say goodbye to your surroundings, as we will never see them again—win or lose. Go now," he said, dismissing them. "We leave immediately after sundown."

The Ignis cheered as they made their way back to their

rooms. I began to follow them out, only for Valerie to stop me.

"Not us," she said. "We've been asked to stay."

My body went cold. "What for?"

"He didn't say."

"Um . . . okay," I muttered, though it was definitely *not* okay. I felt like I might throw up, but I was out of excuses.

So, I hung back, placing myself behind Valerie as all the Ignis left except for those who would fight: Levi, Aiden, Seraphina, Fintan, Zoran, Fiametta, Iri, Kai, and about twenty others whose names I didn't know. The only ones who seemed to not belong were Ren, Cora, and I, and Fintan didn't fail to point it out.

"What is *she* doing here?" he asked Nur, pointing at Cora. "What is she gonna do? Give them boils?"

Seraphina laughed, and I couldn't help but chuckle.

"You have no reason to be here either, Ventus," Aiden said to me.

"They're both with me," Valerie snapped before turning back to Nur. "I wanted to ask if you'd allow Cora to fight with us as opposed to staying behind with the rest."

Seraphina scoffed. "Why the hell would he do that? That's suicide."

"I appreciate the input, but I believe I asked Nur," Valerie said.

Nur looked at Cora. "Why do you need a Natura to speak on your behalf?"

Cora gave a deep bow. "She's earned your respect. Her words hold weight."

"And yours don't?"

Cora blinked, unsure of how to respond.

Nur continued, "I can't stop you if you want to fight, but you have to be capable of holding your own. I don't want anyone, like your friend there," he said, nodding towards Valerie, "risking their lives because you couldn't handle the heat."

Cora nodded. "That's not a problem. I am more than capable of fending for myself."

"Let's hope so," Nur said before clearing his throat. "Now, the reason I asked you all to stay behind . . . I'm well aware tensions have been high. I know you all find it difficult to trust someone that isn't your kind," he said, mainly towards the Ignis, "but we can't be divided. Out there, we're not from opposing factions but a team working towards the same goal. So I need you all to watch Levi and Valerie's backs just like I expect them to watch yours. It's the only way we'll win."

They regarded each other cagily, but not one of them said a word in response.

Though I was relieved the impromptu meeting hadn't resulted in an ambush, I had told Calder he had a week. I needed to buy the Icis more time, so I cleared my throat and slowly raised my hand.

Nur's brows furrowed. "Yes, Eren?"

I forced myself to keep my eyes on Nur, though I could feel everyone else's on me, especially Levi's. "I don't think this is a good idea," I said, but my voice shook. I cleared my throat again. "It's too soon. Surely, our chances would be greater if we took more time to plan. Maybe we could negotiate a new treaty?"

"We need to strike now while we have the element of surprise," Nur said. "And this isn't a discussion. It's a presentation." I began to protest, but Nur raised his hand to stop me. "I've crunched the numbers, Eren. We will fight tomorrow."

I nodded feebly. There was nothing I could do to change Nur's mind when my opinion meant nothing to any of them.

"We need to escort everyone safely through the lake," Nur directed. "Steadily and quietly."

"Eren and I will go last," Valerie said. "Since he hasn't been evoked, the lake will still burn for him."

Levi pushed himself off the wall he had been leaning against. "He'll stay behind with me. I'll make sure he goes through just fine."

I glanced towards Levi, and my stomach dropped.

I knew then, by the look in Levi's eyes, that this abrupt call to action was all his doing, and it was only a matter of time before he told Valerie.

I was no longer safe here. I needed to find my way back to the Icis before whatever Levi had planned for me came to pass.

I struggled to conceal my shock, which made me one of the last ones out, and I cursed at myself for not keeping up with Valerie's group. I trailed in the back, and just as I had feared, Levi stopped in his tracks, turning to face me.

We were alone in the hallway with the others too far to see or hear us. I could feel the blood pulsing through my veins as the adrenaline surged through my body, but I couldn't run—that would only confirm Levi's suspicions. I had to stand my ground and *deny, deny, deny*.

Levi's eyes scrutinized me hard. "Be careful with me, Eren," he said. "That's not a threat. It's a warning."

I swallowed hard. It took everything I had to keep my face composed and my feet in place when all I wanted to do was run. Levi *knew*.

Fortunately, he left before my body could break out in hives.

Chapter Fifteen

Even a Worm Will Turn

VALERIE

It took us longer than we expected to get everyone through the lake. Its close proximity to the Icis forced us to move at a snail's pace, but we made up for lost time on the other side; lucky the sun set so early this time of year.

Levi, Eren, Nur, Fintan, and I were the first to get to Hestia's cabin, and I could hardly contain my excitement to see her and Eika again. But, even though Levi insisted Hestia had offered to help of her own volition, part of me still felt guilty for dragging her into our mess.

As we walked to the clearing, Eika was the first to greet us. I could hardly contain my laughter when she pounced out of the trees and rubbed against my legs, making Fintan squeal like a pig. Everyone, except for Levi, kept their anxious eyes on her until we finally reached the cabin.

The cabin door opened, and Hestia emerged, standing tall.

Nur stepped ahead of our group and gave Hestia a

slight bow of his head as a sign of respect. "We thank you for offering your land and your assistance," he said.

Hestia cleared her throat and waved for him to straighten himself out. "I've lived alone in these here woods since I lost me clan. The lad and lassie," she said, motioning towards Levi and me, "they be the only kin I have now, so this be my fight as much as yers."

The look on Hestia's face as she spoke broke my heart. I closed the distance between us, wrapping my arms around her in a tight hug. None of us deserved her kindness.

Hestia was stiff at first—we had never hugged or even touched before. But, after a moment, she relaxed and hugged me in return. "Now, now, Valerie. I don't want to embarrass meself in front of yer folk," she said, her voice deep with emotion.

I chuckled and let go. "Sorry."

She smiled at me before turning to Nur, motioning to the area around her. "It's all yers."

THE IGNIS, WHO ARRIVED IN WAVES, WATCHED IN WONDER as I got to work on the woods. I knew having them witness what I could do would come to bite me in the ass later, but I couldn't afford to hold back now.

I planned to make the woods thicker to give us plenty of places to hide and ambush, so I focused on turning the bare trees into lush covers. With Hestia's help, we strategically picked out several nonnative seeds and planted them to add to the foliage—cannas, elephant's ears, Hosta's, and even banana trees; anything and everything I could think of with paddle-like leaves to give us ample cover. I sprinkled in false azalea's, too, whose leaves produced a skunky smell when crushed, advising the Ignis who watched to avoid them, so they could gauge the Icis' movements by the scent.

An hour passed, and I had transformed the once plain Alaskan woods into a dense tropical jungle. The Ignis walked around, studying and admiring the plants, having never seen most of them before in their entire lives.

"So, this is what you can do?" Zoran asked in amazement, ruffling my hair.

I smiled at him, pointed in the direction of the fruit, and he ran over to gorge himself in response. Cora still waited by the lake for her turn to come over, and Levi had wandered off to make his own arrangements, whatever those might be, so I took a seat next to Hestia to decompress.

"Where's George?" I asked her.

"I sent the lad back to his clan. He's not prepared fer what's ahead."

"Ah, I see."

He would only get in the way, I thought and snickered, but then again . . . that was hardly fair of me.

George, and everyone he loved, lived tranquil lives in the Origin. Not oppressed or tyrannized by the Icis in any way, shape, or form. He had everything to lose and nothing to gain if he fought with us.

"The lad," Hestia said, "he asked that I tell ya he feels wretched over what he said. He hopes yer forgive 'em."

I nodded. "Because he thinks I won't make it."

Hestia balked at the words, reaching out to pacify me, but Nur called me over to where he and Fintan stood before she could respond.

"It's fine, Hestia. It's fine," I said, patting her hand. "You could tell him that I forgive him."

Her eyes met mine as I stood, and though I noticed

them welling up, I made my way over to Nur and Fintan anyway. Painfully aware of how difficult I found it to climb out of, I couldn't afford to entertain George's grim outlook.

"I need you two to search the perimeter for any sign of humans," Nur said once I had reached him. "The last thing we need is a sighting, sending a swarm of conspiracy theorists our way."

"Does this need to be a group project?" Fintan asked.

"Well, if you do see any, it would look suspicious if you're roaming the woods alone."

"I could just check from the treetops," I offered, equally unenthusiastic about partnering with Fintan. "I won't be seen there. We don't need to go together."

"So they could think they've walked onto the set of a live-action Tarzan?" Fintan asked.

"Did I not just say I wouldn't be seen? Maybe if you'd—"

Fintan cut me off. "Consider using common sense once in a while."

"Don't interrupt me when I'm speaking," I snapped.

"Hey!" Nur shouted. "What the hell is the matter with you two? Talk. One of you," he added after neither of us responded.

Fintan veered his head to the side in defiance.

"Fine. I'll go," I said. "I get that I'm not an Ignis. None of you have ever let me forget that. But Fintan has treated me like trash since the moment we met, so, frankly, I don't feel comfortable bounding through the woods with him alone."

Fintan scoffed. "Look," he said, speaking only to Nur. "I had to get used to Levi. We all did. Hell, I can even admit that he's part of the reason we're alive today. But I have no reason to get used to her. I mean, is there a

Ventus-Icis hybrid that we have to just be okay with, too? When does it stop?"

"What have I ever done to upset you, Fintan? Exist? You talk like I had a say in that—like I chose to be here. If it was within my power, I would have never met you. Trust me."

"That's beside the point! It's because of you that we're even in this situation at all. Don't remember? Well, let me jog your memory," he said, taking steps in my direction before continuing.

"We're only about to fight the Icis now because you came along and fucked everything up. Without you, we'd still be living our perfectly peaceful lives in the cave. You're the one pushing us to risk our lives solely for the sake of one elemental that isn't even our kind only because it happens to be your brother."

I let out a mirthless laugh. "I don't call the shots here. Nur does. And I don't see you berating Levi every chance you get when, with your logic, we wouldn't be here if he hadn't had the nerve to exist either."

"Unlike you, he doesn't walk around our home like he owns the place."

"It's because you're afraid of him, right?" I asked, closing the distance between us. "Maybe I should make you afraid of me, too, so you'd leave me the fuck alone."

"Do it," he goaded. "I'd love to see you try."

Just as I prepared myself to do *just* that, bright blue flames flared between us, making us both jump back.

"Watch yourself," Levi said to Fintan, positioning himself between us.

"She provoked me!"

"And you provoked *me*."

Fintan glared at Levi and, in a burst of sheer frustration, hurled a fireball at a tree, igniting it. Nur snapped at Kai and another Ignis to extinguish the fire.

"This is the bullshit I'm talking about!" Fintan shouted, turning to the crowd of Ignis that had formed around us. "I knew from the moment I saw her that she was going to be a fucking problem. Now, look at the crossbreeds banding together. You're all delusional if you think it'll stop here. Mark my words."

"Distance yourself, Fintan," Levi cautioned. "Before I make you."

The now red-faced Fintan visibly shook, and the air tensed around him.

Seraphina walked up to him, whispering something into his ear—hopefully, something to calm him. But she glared at me from the corner of her eyes, so probably not.

I'd had enough, and now, the only thing keeping me from decking Seraphina was my fondness for Ren. How was she even able to bag her? Ren, though annoying at times, was kind. Seraphina? Decidedly not.

Levi's expression dared Fintan to continue, but Nur interjected with, "Go, cool off," and Fintan stalked off into the woods, with Seraphina trailing behind him.

"Well done, Valerie," Nur muttered, pinching the bridge of his nose.

I scoffed. "You're kidding."

"I'm not known for my humor," he said. "You're not making it any easier on yourself by stooping to his level."

I watched him in disbelief. How could he say that? I did nothing wrong. Tears flooded my eyes, and I left before he could see them spill, having been humiliated enough for one day.

I walked past Cora, who had just arrived, and I didn't stop.

"I love what you've done to the place," she said when

she saw me, her face full of admiration as she took everything in. "I'm usually more of an 'indoor girl' myself, but this is nice."

"Could you have taken any longer, or were you aiming to miss the fight altogether?" I asked while I watched Levi have a heated discussion with Nur, wishing he would have followed me instead.

Her eyes widened. "Do you want to talk about whatever's put you in this charming mood?"

I slumped to the ground against the trunk of a catalpa, burying my face in my hands.

"She and Fintan fought," Zoran answered for me.

She gasped. "Was it physical?"

"I wish," he muttered. "He would've gotten his ass handed to him."

Someone sat by me. "Don't let Fintan get to you, Val," Cora said. "He can't help it. Being a dick is Fintan's sole personality trait."

I laughed. It was no secret Fintan was a rude and petulant man by nature. If someone put a gun to my head and asked me to name three positive qualities Fintan had, tell my family I love them. But what hurt me the most was that a lot of what he said rang true; it's why I fought back the way I did. I didn't want to admit that I was, undeniably, the catalyst for this whole affair.

And should things go wrong, I would be the only one to blame.

CHAPTER SIXTEEN

Night Owls

"We won't all fit into this tiny cabin," Eren griped. He appeared to be in yet another one of his crabby moods —what a shocker.

"There's a secret bunker underneath," I said.

"Why didn't you mention that to me before?"

"It wouldn't have been much of a secret if I did."

"You just love keeping me out of the loop," he muttered.

Exasperated, I threw my hands in the air. "What difference could knowing this have possibly made, Eren?"

"Forget it," he snapped and stalked off into the woods.

Levi caught the interaction and shot me an inquisitive look.

I shrugged. His guess was as good as mine.

I couldn't recall a time when Eren ever acted this way back home, and I couldn't fathom why he chose to now, but I'd had enough. I needed to focus on what lay ahead and not the field of landmines surrounding his feelings. They would just need to wait.

It was half-past eight by the time we finished preparations and settled down to rest. The Ignis slept in Hestia's bunker while Hestia, Eren, and I had the cabin to ourselves. Levi insisted he'd sleep outside to keep a lookout.

After our squabble, Eren didn't speak to me again, leaving me with a groundless sense of guilt. I tossed and turned restlessly until I finally managed to chuck those thoughts away. I was nodding off, finally having gotten used to Hestia's thunderous snores, when I sensed a dark figure looming over me.

"Ah!" I screamed, clutching at my sheets.

The figure giggled quietly. When my eyes adjusted to the darkness, I noticed who it was.

"Shit, Cora!" I hissed, my head snapping to Hestia and Eren, who had miraculously remained unbothered. "We'll both die young if you wake me up like that again."

She tried to quiet her laugh but failed. "Oh my god. Your face was priceless."

"What the hell do you want?"

"I can't sleep," she said when she managed to compose herself.

"Maybe because you're sneaking around scaring people. Have you considered that?"

"I need to take my mind off these nerves, but I don't know this area. I've never been to the Origin, but you have. Come with me!"

"Come with you, where?"

"Is there a bar around here?"

"I can't go anywhere like this, Cora! I look awful."

"Never stopped you before."

I rolled my eyes at her. "Nice."

"Please," she begged, shaking her clasped hands in the

air. "I've only ever seen them in movies, but they look like so much fun!"

I only thought about it for a brief moment before agreeing. There was no telling whether we'd get another chance, and everyone deserved to experience a shitty bar at least once in their lives. "I guess we could try to find one," I sighed.

"Good, because I could really use some liquid courage right about now."

I considered waking Eren so he could tag along but decided sleep may do his mood better than a night out with the girls. It wouldn't be fair to subject Cora to his hostile attitude, so only Cora and I snuck out of the cabin and made our way to the Jeep. I guided her through the longer route, so we'd stumbled upon Levi, who was leaning against a tree, seemingly asleep.

"Where are you going?" Levi asked, his eyes still closed.

Cora jumped in surprise. I didn't.

"We're going to a bar," I whispered. "Come with us."

"We're fighting a war tomorrow," he said, his eyes opening slowly to look at us. "There's no time for that."

"He's right," Cora said to me, her determination crumbling under Levi's stare. "Let's go back. I don't mind."

"That's sweet of you," I said to her. "But considering you already went to the trouble of waking me, it's very unconvincing." I turned to Levi and pouted. "Come on, Levi. Just for a few hours!"

He watched us for a moment before sighing and getting to his feet. "A couple of hours tops."

I beamed at Cora, who made a face at me. She hadn't expected Levi to join us, but I couldn't tell her that I had chosen this particular path for this very reason. Or that I would need liquid courage, too, for what I had planned for tonight.

IT TOOK AN HOUR TO FIND A BAR SINCE THE CLOSEST TOWN happened to be Nenana, a tiny village of less than four hundred that hosted only a handful of businesses, but low and behold, we found Moochers, a quaint bar that sat unassumingly off the road. We only spotted it because its moss-colored wood panels stood out against the pale white of the snow.

Before we got out of the Jeep, I searched the trunk for any article of clothing that wasn't a dull tan. There wasn't, so I rolled up our sleeves and tied a knot on the side of our shirts to give them some shape. I hoped it would make us appear less ridiculous. Then, I opened the glove compartment and placed sunglasses on Cora while I was at it.

"What are these for?" she asked.

"Unless you want the patrons to run out screaming, 'the end of the world is upon us,' we have to cover up these eyes."

"They wouldn't be wrong," Levi muttered.

"Yeah, well, it doesn't do them any good to know," I said.

As we stepped out of the car, I caught a whiff of something foul and realized Cora was about to step into a puddle of vomit someone had left in the parking lot. "Cora, don't move," I warned.

"What?" she asked, shuffling her feet which in turn led her straight into the puddle. "Oh, *gross!*"

Levi and I keeled over in laughter.

"I told you not to move!" I roared.

"Couldn't you have told me there was barf?"

"If I told you, you would have bathed in it."

Cora flicked me off as she dragged her foot across the

pavement. "What a great way to start the night," she miffed.

THE BAR WAS AT FULL CAPACITY. ALMOST AS THOUGH THEY knew it could very well be their last night alive. We moved sideways between the billiard tables and the crowd, nearly knocking over the drink of a girl who was too preoccupied with the chime of a new text to make room for us. The patrons eyed us curiously, probably trying to crack whether Cora, with her sunglasses inside a bar after sundown, could possibly be a celebrity in hiding. Cora laughed when I mentioned it.

"Please, no pictures," Cora said to a man as she walked past him, and we giggled at his bewildered expression.

We went straight to a spot by the bar, waiting while a waitress cleared the table and wiped it down for us.

Once gone, Levi ordered tequila shots from the bartender, and she was *striking*. With her come-hither expression and tits pushed nearly to her chin, I was sure her tips would reach an exorbitant amount tonight. She smiled sphinx-like at Levi as she placed his order on the bar.

Levi knocked one of the shots back and motioned for us to have the others.

Cora squealed in excitement and downed hers, her face contorting as the burn of the shot made its way down her throat. She sucked in a breath through her teeth while she held in a gag. "Your turn," Cora said to me.

"I'm okay. You can have mine," I said. "You're not exactly selling the experience."

"Are you really okay?" Levi wondered.

"You still bother asking her? Valerie could have her

intestines trailing behind her and still swear she's fine," Cora teased, only to slap a hand over her mouth, shocked at having spoken to Levi that way.

But Levi smiled. "That's healthy."

Cora eased at the sight of it, her shoulders relaxing.

Their pithy banter warmed me—even if it was at my expense. I didn't want to be a Debbie-Downer, so I called the bartender over to me. "Hey, could you make me the fruitiest drink imaginable?"

She raised a brow but nodded and handed me a mysterious blue concoction. I raised the glass to Cora and Levi and took a generous gulp while I held my breath, happy to find that it tasted like pure sugar with only a hint of rum. "Perfect," I said to the sphinx. "Thank you."

It was the burn of the straight liquor that I wouldn't be able to stand. I didn't need to be reminded of anything right now. Tonight was about enjoying ourselves, and we only had a few hours.

"Anytime," she said in her sultry voice, stealing one last glance at Levi—who, to my delight, didn't return her attentions.

CORA DRAGGED ME OUT TO THE DANCE FLOOR AFTER HER fifth shot. We danced without any particular skill or grace, but we danced joyfully. It felt liberating to be in a room where no one feared or loathed me, where I could be as silly as I'd like. And Cora was over the moon. She swayed back and forth to "Girls Just Want to Have Fun" by Cyndi Lauper and doubled over cackling when she realized she had spilled some of her drink on a man behind her.

After a couple more upbeat eighties anthems, Cyndi Lauper returned with "True Colors," and those on the dance floor paired up to slow dance. Cora looked around wistfully, nibbling on her bottom lip, disappointed at the idea of having to leave the dance floor.

I set my drink aside and took her hand as she turned to leave. "Dance with me?"

"People will think we're together," she said.

"So what?"

She watched me for a moment to be sure I meant it, and then her whole face lit up. "I'd love to."

I placed one hand on the small of her back and held Cora's hand with the other, moving at a gentle pace. She looked nervous, fumbling with the steps and landing on my toes. She glanced around to check if anyone caught her awkward slip-up, and it was then that I realized Cora had never danced this way before, and I vowed to make this moment memorable.

"It's okay," I whispered. "Just watch me."

She shot me a rueful smile and focused on mirroring my movements.

I didn't move us around too much at first to avoid over-whelming Cora and kept us in a tight circle instead. But, soon, we were floating around the dance floor like naturals. She beamed at me, a giggle escaping her lips as we let our worries about what lay ahead fade away and cherished our now.

A few minutes later, the song came to an end, its notes trailing off. We waited only to hear "Africa" by Toto take its place.

"Oh, I love this song!" Cora exclaimed, reverting back to her wild, featherbrained dancing.

I laughed, grabbed my glass from where I had left it, and glanced at the bar to see Levi watching us intently, a stirring stick playing in the corner of his mouth.

"I'm gonna get us another," I said, raising my glass to Cora.

She nodded vigorously, lost in the music.

I moved through the dancing bodies, dodging as many as I could when I felt a hand on my back. I turned to see a man, around his late thirties, smiling—the cloying scent of his cologne bearing down on me. He said something I didn't quite catch over a toast the group behind us made, but I deduced he attempted to lure me into dancing with him. I declined his offer but gave him a smile to ease the snub.

When I turned back, Levi seemed to be sizing the man up, his jaw clenched and brows furrowed.

I bit my lip to hide just how much that pleased me. "You're looking real good over here," I teased. "So brooding and mysterious."

His expression fully transformed as he took me in, and he smiled his big, nose-crinkling smile—my favorite. "Stop," he gushed. "I'm melting."

"Why don't you join us?"

"I'm not nearly drunk enough to dance yet."

"Can I get another round over here?" I called out to the bartender.

"Are you trying to take advantage of me?"

"Why? Would you like me to?" I asked in return, batting my lashes at him.

He watched me for a moment—his lips quirking into a radiant smile. "With a face like yours, who could say no?"

"I know," I sighed. "Like the Sun, you aren't supposed to look directly at me."

Levi chuckled but glanced down at his drink. "You know . . . you make me really happy, Valerie," he said, and I could almost swear his cheeks burned red, though, with the only illumination in the bar coming from atmospheric twinkling lights, I couldn't be sure. "I don't remember ever laughing as much as I have since I met you."

I rolled my eyes to distract him from my irrepressible answering smile.

"I'm serious," he insisted. "You make me feel . . . *lighter*. I don't know. Maybe I am drunk."

Seeing him look so flustered made my heart swell, and I was about to assure him the feeling was mutual, but he continued.

"I just find it amazing how, even with everything you've been through, you still find humor everywhere you go."

"It's a defense mechanism," I muttered, laughing.

"Maybe. But it's admirable."

Our eyes met, and, for a while, we simply gazed at each other. No words, but having an entire conversation just the same. Levi's eyes locked onto mine with an intensity I couldn't escape, even if I wished to. As it happened, I didn't care to look anywhere else, but the universe had other plans for us.

"You never came back," Cora whined, pulling on my arm. "Come on. I need to use the bathroom."

Levi laughed at my outstretched hand as she dragged me away from him, but I caught the flicker of sadness in his expression over the loss of our moment, one that mirrored my own.

CORA AND I WALKED DOWN A DINGY HALLWAY, PAST A PAIR of flashing gambling machines, and into the ladies' room. A group of girls stood gossiping in front of an aged mirror as they fixed their makeup, so we locked ourselves into the furthermost stall. Cora placed her sunglasses over her head before squatting over the toilet.

"Can I give you some advice?" she asked once the band of giggling girls had left.

I laughed. "I'd love to hear advice from the woman struggling to balance herself over a toilet seat."

"Be careful with Levi," she said, ignoring my jab. "I've seen the way he looks at you."

I froze, startled to discover we hadn't been as discreet as we thought.

"If he was a Natura, then no biggie," she continued. "You'd just pop out a few earth benders. But two impurities? No one knows, and that's the problem."

I didn't know what to say, so naturally, I deflected. "Your ability to jump from 'making eyes at someone' to 'babies' is remarkable."

"It may be a leap, but it's the leap they'd all make. The Ignis would never approve."

"I don't recall asking for approval," I snapped and instantly regretted it. "I don't want to argue over hypotheticals," I added in a softer tone.

"I don't want to argue at all. I'm only looking out for you."

"I know. And I appreciate that—no matter how crazy you sound. But, while we're dishing unsolicited advice, I have something I'd like to say, too."

"By all means," she said as she washed her hands.

I couldn't find a way to word what I wanted to say, so I cut straight to the point and went with, "Don't fight tomorrow."

She groaned. "Valerie . . . We've talked about this. This isn't about making a name for myself."

"I know, but—"

"Look," she interrupted, rubbing her damp hands onto her jeans. "Let's settle this now." She took something out of her pocket, the tiny magic eight ball I gifted her, and closed her eyes as she shook her fist. "Will I survive the fight tomorrow? No. Better yet—will I kick ass tomorrow?" she asked the ball. She opened her palm, and her eyes narrowed as she strained to read the lettering on the die. "'My sources say no.' Okay. Scratch that," she mumbled.

"Please, Cora," I begged. "I get that you want to be with your sisters, but you don't have to put yourself in harm's way when there are more than enough capable people handling this. Why do you insist on fighting when you aren't meant to? Do you have so little faith in us?"

"Do you expect me to sit on the sidelines while my two prepubescent sisters jeopardize their lives for me?" she asked, fidgeting with her bracelet. She peered down at it, her expression sobering. "This isn't much. In fact, it's rather ugly," she said, brushing her thumb over the chain. "I only kept it because it belonged to my mother."

We stood in silence, neither knowing how to proceed until Cora's face lit with a determination that rivaled my own. "The Icis killed my parents, Valerie. So, yes, I'm going to fight, and you can't tell me you wouldn't do the same. Maybe if more felt the way I did, then I wouldn't have to explain to a seven-year-old that she might need to use her self-combusting ethos for the good of her faction even though it would kill her. I'll be damned if I let my ethos determine the rest of my life. And if I die," she added, placing the ridiculous sunglasses back on her face, "then at least I'll die with a modicum of dignity."

Though the idea left a sinking feeling in my chest, if it meant this much to Cora, then I had to support her. I would just have to make it my mission to protect her. I sighed and approached her with my arms open wide.

She tensed. "What are you doing?"

"I'm giving you a hug," I said, wrapping them around her.

"Why?"

"Just lean into it, Cora. It's okay. Unclench your fists."

After a moment, she did. When at last she relaxed, she wedged her face into the crook of my neck and gave me a tight squeeze in return. She seemed to need the hug just as much as I did.

"Okay," I said, breaking away. "Let's head back before Levi thinks we ditched him."

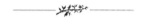

WE RETURNED TO THE UNRULIEST OF SIGHTS.

Levi and a boy, who just barely gained entrance here, were on a modest karaoke stage in the back of the bar, jumping to the beat of a song while a crowd around the platform cheered them on.

Cora gasped, a hard laugh escaping her lips.

"Oh no," I said, my eyes growing wide.

He sang along to "The Promise" by When in Rome with an overabundance of passion but regrettably off-key. It's no secret that being tone-deaf and drunk is a notoriously bad combination, but it somehow made Levi that much more endearing. He pointed at us when we came into view, making the entire bar turn to see who we were.

Cora shielded her face with her hands at the unwanted attention, but I was too entranced at the sight of him to do the same.

Levi yelled the words to the chorus into the wind. He had the entire bar singing along with him, but his eyes were on me, and my pulse raced as I took in the lyrics he so fervently sang in my direction.

I knew then, as my heart nearly exploded in my chest, that I was absolutely falling for Levi—and I wasn't the only one doing the falling.

The crowd erupted into applause when the song ended. They chanted for another, but Levi had already hopped off the stage to meet up with us.

"Hey," he said, breathless but smiling from ear to ear.

"That was . . . really something," I said between giggles.

"It's the only song they've played all night that I recognized. It just called to me."

"You've got a healthy belt," Cora teased.

I nudged her with my elbow, recounting the time my brothers and I organized a mock concert for my father and how Eren decided to sing "American Pie" by Don McLean of all songs. The three of us sat there for its entire duration, trying not to laugh. It was torture.

Cora chuckled at the story, but Levi remained deadpan.

"That song is nearly ten minutes long," I clarified. "He chose one of the longest songs to ever exist."

"I know the song," he said.

"Oh, okay. I guess it's one of those 'you had to be there' moments."

He didn't respond.

"I have feelings, Levi."

"You're fine. Sorry. It was funny."

"What is it?" I asked, trying to decipher the bizarre look in his eyes.

He didn't answer right away, taking a moment to consider his response. "It's nothing," he decided.

"Fine," I said, shrugging. "We should probably close out the tab now."

I made my way to the bar with Levi trailing behind me.

"Something's up," I said, shooting him a side-eye. "What is it?"

"I know what's waiting for us when we get back," he

said, taking a deep breath to steady himself. "But I feel so high right now, and I never want to come down."

"The night isn't over," I said. "We can still enjoy it."

"Not in the way I'd like to."

The look he gave me made my breath catch in my throat. I wanted nothing more than to hear precisely how he had hoped to enjoy it. But the reason he couldn't presented itself on its own.

Cora wiggled herself between us. "Are we ready to go?" she asked, flashing a tight smile at me. She knew exactly what she had walked into.

Levi let out a short, humorless laugh before announcing he'd start the car.

"As ready as I'll ever be," I answered her, watching him go while Cora's warning still echoed in my mind.

TENSIONS WERE HIGH AS LEVI DROVE US BACK. I KEPT MY eyes glued to the window and my hands on my lap, fully aware that Cora scrutinized our every move from the backseat.

When we finally parked near the edge of the woods leading to Hestia's cabin, Levi's eyes remained on the road ahead but, as I began to open the door, he rested his hand on my thigh.

It was an invitation, like the one I had given him in the river.

"Do you remember the way?" I asked Cora, who stood fumbling next to the car with the knot I had made to her shirt.

"Yeah, it's just a straight shot down," she said, not yet realizing why I had asked.

"Good. We'll catch up with you later."

Her eyes flew to mine. "Why?"

"I'll catch up in a bit," I said, hard and deliberate.

She looked at me for a moment and sighed. "Make good choices," she whispered before making her way through the woods.

Levi started the car back up. We drove in silence for a few minutes before he picked an isolated spot concealed from the road and cut the engine. A song with soft melodies played on the radio, one I had never heard before, or at least I didn't think I had. I couldn't be sure. My mind couldn't focus on anything besides the fact that I was entirely alone with Levi—miles away from another soul. I reached over to him, and he held my hand, tracing the lines on my palm.

"What did you do to me?" he asked, and though his words were heavy, his tone was soft.

The question, simple as it was, made my stomach flip. And, though it comforted me to hear I wasn't alone in feeling the way I did, it also terrified me.

What if Levi shared only a fraction of my affections for him? I didn't want to embarrass myself by assuming Levi meant more than his words implied. I mean, he had been drinking, after all. And even if he felt as much as I hoped he did, would it be right of me to encourage him? I couldn't brush off Cora's words of caution simply because they didn't suit me.

But tonight, we were alone. There were no Ignis around to chastise any questionable decisions we made, and we had no guarantee we would ever get another chance to act on our impulses. So could we truly be blamed if we indulged in our selfish desires, if only for one night?

I jumped out of my seat and maneuvered myself over the armrests. When Levi registered my intentions, he

gripped my hips and hoisted me onto his lap until I strad-
dled him.

We were now at eye level—so close that I could see the
crinkled lines around his eyes, those mesmerizing sky-blue
eyes. The prominent contrast between them and his dark
hair captivated me. I took in every intricate detail of his
face, enthralled with the way the moon lit his features, as I
rested on the lap of the most striking man I had ever seen.

"I meant to ask you the same thing," I whispered.

Levi's pupils flared in response. He held my face
between his hands, drawing me in until his lips found mine.
They were soft and inviting, but I yearned for more. I
parted my lips, and he swept his tongue inside my mouth,
morphing the kiss into one relying solely on instinct, and
the sweet taste of bourbon on his tongue intoxicated me.

His hands pulled my shirt over my head with his
following less than a second after, making us break our kiss,
but only for a moment before he found my lips again.

Now, with my chest bare in front of him, his hands
made their way to my breasts, cradling them. Levi's mouth
traveled down my neck and chest, leaving cold, dewy
imprints along the way. I let out an involuntary shiver when
Levi's mouth reached my breast and suckled me, his
tongue drawing circles around my hardening nipples.

I gasped as every action on my breast I felt below. I
squirmed against Levi, the movement causing my back to
hit the steering wheel hard, and the honk that followed
startled me. He laughed at my reaction, but the rumble of
his laughter against my breast only excited me more.

With one swift move, he pulled the lever on the side of
the seat, flattened it, and positioned me so that I laid on my
back while he hovered above.

My hands traced the muscles on Levi's smooth chest
before his mouth came down on me again, but this still

wasn't enough. I needed *all* of him. I fumbled with the buttons on his jeans and cursed when I couldn't figure how to undo them.

But Levi couldn't wait either, so he took over. He expertly tugged our jeans off, and my thoughts turned almost feral as I took him in. Levi was fully erect and fully *packed*. I took a deep breath to calm myself as he positioned himself over me again and gently pressed his hips against mine, allowing me to register his length between my legs.

Levi's eyes bore into mine, his pupils dilating, and my heart raced in anticipation.

I had never felt so seen in my entire life. And yet, I didn't feel remotely nervous or self-conscious like I thought I might. I felt safe to release my inhibitions because he made me feel . . . accepted. And not just accepted, but *desired*.

He didn't break his gaze as he reached down and placed himself at my entrance, and I nearly cried out when, instead of diving in, he rubbed himself against me —his breath quickening as he felt it glide. I had been ready since we parked, and now I ached for it. My eyes rolled to the back of my head as he stroked against me again, savoring its effect on me.

"Please, Levi," I begged. "*Please.*"

He drew in a long breath, and with that, he slid into me, not requiring any further persuasion. We moaned in concert as he pushed further into me still, though slowly to allow my body to adjust to his girth. And damn, did it need adjusting. I arched my back at the feeling of fullness as he worked his way in deeper and deeper.

"*God damn,*" Levi breathed as I wrapped myself around him. He lowered himself onto me, his mouth impatiently coaxing mine.

As our kiss intensified, I lifted my legs over the steering

wheel, placed my hands on his lower back, and pulled him into me hard. My eyes shut, and I let out an involuntary whimper as I felt his base slam against me.

Levi cursed, pausing to collect himself before moving again. His pace remained slow at first, sensual. It was incredible. I gripped him as he made his way out, my body urging him to stay, which only caused him to plunge back into me again, only now with a vengeance.

The tension rose until soon his thrusts turned feverish —his grunts and moans pervading my senses. The sounds Levi made drove me wild, and I appreciated how he wasn't afraid to show just how much he enjoyed me.

I could hear Levi's breath quicken, but instead of finishing, he paused. One of his hands reached behind my lower back, raising me up to him while the other held his weight to keep from crushing me. Once my back was arched, Levi's mouth moved down to my breast, where he latched on fiercely.

I gasped, thankful he noted my reaction to that before.

Then, he picked up the pace again. Levi pounded into me with hard but deliberate thrusts, grunting even with my breast filling his mouth.

I cried out, feeling how close I was, and just then, his teeth clamped onto my breast, and the sweet pain paired with his calculated assault made my body go haywire, and I came so hard that I shook beneath him.

Levi's thrusts became sporadic, and he fought to keep himself from falling onto me as he lost all control—filling me as he finished, too.

When our bodies finally came down from the high, he let out a harsh breath and carefully lowered his head onto my chest, his length still pulsating inside me.

It was a long time before either of us could speak. Levi tapped his fingers tenderly against my chest to the beat of my heart as it struggled to return to its usual rhythm. Though we were covered in sweat and . . . other things, neither of us made any effort to move—both blissfully happy to stay just the way we were.

He kissed my collarbone before propping himself up to look at me. "How do you feel?"

I gave him a lazy smile. "I've never felt better."

"Good," Levi said, a mischievous smile on his lips. His fingers parted me, massaging the natural lubricant we created just moments ago back into me. "I'm not done with you yet."

I was playing with fire, and I didn't care—even if it burned me.

Chapter Seventeen

Swan Song

An all-encompassing sense of dread fell over the campsite the following morning. The Ignis remained silent as they picked at the fruit Hestia laid out for them, their expressions foreboding. They left behind the enthusiasm Nur incited during his speech in the cave, along with the rest of their belongings. Their track record didn't necessarily scream "success story," so who could blame them?

Though I tried my best to exude a positive attitude, I couldn't help but share their trepidation. After all, I was no expert on my craft. I was no seasoned fighter. And I was also hungover, exhausted, and sore, but I didn't care too much about that. I wouldn't have given up the night before for anything in the world. I had never felt more alive.

Cora looked withdrawn as she walked past me, or maybe she was just hungover, too. "I watched the sunrise this morning," she said to me. "Couldn't sleep."

"How was it?" I asked.

"Average."

I chuckled. "Remind me to thank you for convincing

me to go on a bender the night before a war. You're a terrible influence."

"You didn't put up much of a fight, from what I remember," she said. "But, honestly, I don't regret it one bit. Last night reminded me what I was fighting for, the chance to do that again."

"It's a date."

She smiled. "You betcha."

"Any word from Nur?"

"He's waiting to hear back from Aiden and Seraphina," Cora said. "They left a few hours ago to do the deed."

They had been instructed to let the Icis know where to find us. I had no idea how they planned to do so but trusted Seraphina to get creative.

Cora and I thought to meditate before they arrived in order to harness our chi but spent the entire time peeking to ensure we each had our eyes closed, only to burst into laughter when our eyes met. I clamped my hands over my mouth and urged her to do the same to avoid coming off as insensitive with everything going on around us.

As I accompanied Cora to the fruit platers, I saw Levi speaking with Nur, and my cheeks turned pink, remembering how we spent our night. After our second go, we were so exhausted that we fell asleep entwined in the driver's seat and had to rush back when we woke only five hours later.

Nur approached us, and my heart raced to see Levi follow. I focused on keeping my face as composed as his when we made eye contact, but then Levi licked his lips, and my self-control crumbled. All I could think about was how much I wanted his lips and tongue on *me*.

"We're going to have everyone in the cabin during the fight, Cora," Nur said. "I'll need you to stay here with Fiametta to defend it. We'll do everything in our power to keep them from the cabin, but if anyone slips past us, then you two will be our last line of defense. Under no circumstances can they get close enough to enter this cabin. The future of our entire faction sits in one place."

Cora nodded. "Understood."

"Valerie?"

"Yeah?" I asked, breaking my gaze away from Levi, bitting down on his lip, and towards the actual conversation at hand.

"We're going to position ourselves around the outskirts of what you've created here," Nur continued. "We'll rely on you and Hestia to run the perimeter and help where needed."

"Sounds good." I had planned to stay close to Cora and her sisters anyway, so the more leeway Nur gave me, the better.

Just then, Seraphina and Aiden trudged into view, hauling a frenzied metal casing, and it sounded very much like something struggled to escape from within.

"It's done," Aiden said. "They'll be here soon."

"Who's inside?" Nur asked, rushing to help them.

"Pavati."

That captured everyone's attention. Pavati, my only relief during those grueling days, sloshed around in her liquid form, searching for an opening to slip out of while trapped in a steel casing only ten feet away. This was all becoming too real.

"We saw her and figured we could use her as leverage for your brother," Aiden said to me.

I nodded, not knowing whether I should thank or chide them.

"She was a slippery cunt," Seraphina added, slapping the bulky case. "Real sneaky, but not nearly as sneaky as I am."

"Get her inside," Nur ordered, snapping his fingers towards the cabin. "Everyone get in position! The Icis won't hesitate when they realize we have Calder's mate."

The Ignis scattered off to their posts. I searched for Eren, only for a man to tell me he had already scurried into the cabin, and my heart sank. I hoped to hear some encouraging words or at least hug him before the war began, but it was too late for that now.

"Do you have a minute?" Levi asked me.

"From the look of things, that might be all I have."

He didn't laugh. Instead, he led me to a spot behind a banana tree, whose paddle-like leaves gave us a touch of privacy. He held my hands, his eyes piercing into mine. "Keep your feet on the ground and Eika by your side. She'll see the Icis a hundred times before they see her once, so she'll be able to sense if someone is near in time for you to react. I'll do everything I can to keep them away, but if I'm not…successful, use Pavati as leverage."

I nodded. "Right, for the Ignis in the cabin."

"Sure. Them, too."

"Levi, I—"

He placed his fingers over my lips only to remove them before anyone else could see. "We'll see each other after. Tell me then."

I watched Levi disappear into the woods with a consuming sense of dread that left an ache in the back of my throat. One that I couldn't shake.

I didn't have a religious bone in my body, but I didn't care at that moment. I closed my eyes and prayed to whoever would listen, imploring they keep Levi safe and bring him back to me.

Seraphina was the last to leave. She lingered by the cabin door, exchanging a few words with Ren before placing a tender kiss on her lips.

I turned away, not wishing to intrude on their intimate moment. Choosing to dwell on the intimate moments, or the lack thereof, I had with my loved ones instead.

Were we doing the right thing here, or was this a futile act of desperation? No matter how much planning went into this, we were still at a massive disadvantage. The Icis had the numbers and resources. All the Ignis had was determination and two hybrids. One of which had zero experience and an undiagnosed mental condition or two.

I stood by the cabin alone, muttering over the unfairness of our situation under my breath, when I noticed a carpenter ant crawling its way up the trunk of an aspen. I made a wall around it in the form of a triangle with my hands, and the ant panicked—too busy running up and down the sides to consider that it would be free if it would just climb over them.

Maybe all I had to do was leave, and I would be free too. Only the Icis had Grant. Eren, Hestia, Zoran, and Cora were all out there, too.

And Levi. I couldn't leave Levi.

No matter how I spun it, I had no choice but to stay.

Cora emerged from the cabin after settling the Ignis and began to anxiously break apart branches.

"Don't do that," I whispered.

She mouthed "sorry" at me before joining Fiametta behind the cabin.

Eika sauntered over and sat beside me with a blank expression on her face. There wasn't a single thought behind her eyes today—not an inkling of the danger we were in.

Better that way.

The deafening silence made me itch for something to do, so I focused on adding more and more foliage to our immediate surroundings. I covered the cabin's wood paneling with ivy to camouflage it, only to stop when I realized the sounds could potentially attract an Icis to us.

As fear began to set in, I wrapped my arms around my emotional support panther and gave Eika a gentle squeeze, delighted when she didn't object.

Then, out of the blue, I heard the first sounds of violence. It came from far out on the outskirts, and it sounded very much like a wave. I took a deep breath and climbed the aspen to get a better view. Levi insisted I stay grounded, but what help can that be if I can't see?

Once at the top, I surveyed the area and saw a tree ignited in the east. I watched as the forest became lit with fire, only to be subsequently put out by the Icis' attacks. The relentless onslaught had smoke and steam rising over the trees, making it impossible to see through. The canopy would not help as much as I had hoped, but it still offered more protection than if I were to stay on the ground.

AN HOUR PASSED, AND I COULDN'T HELP BUT FEEL powerless. I could hear the war happening all around me, and yet, here I was, sitting in the safety of the treetops. What was the point of a secret weapon if you weren't going to use it? I had to do *something*.

I glanced at the cabin to check on Cora and Fiametta before heading east. They were crouched behind a cluster of ostrich ferns, surveilling the woods, and I had to be sure that was as much excitement as they were going to see.

I didn't dare go on foot. Instead, I had the branches of one tree weave into the next, creating a path for me above, careful to scan the area for any sign of an Icis before growing the limbs since it was impossible to do quietly. Eika followed, slithering behind me.

Then, out of the corner of my eye, I saw a bright flash and turned to see Nur powering up. Right in front of him, a tornado of fire formed, higher than the trees themselves. The fires licked the leaves around them, setting them aflame as Nur propelled the tornado ahead of him and into an unsuspecting Icis.

The Icis had no time to escape or counter. I had no idea what his power even was because Nur completely incinerated him.

Just then, another Icis appeared, having heard his friends' cries, but what he didn't notice was the trail of fire moving unnaturally behind him. This wasn't a remnant of a previous fight; it had a mind of its own.

Nur worked furiously on his next attack. But the Icis, who looked to be summoning a dark cloud from overhead, was fast. Unfortunately for him, the fire creeping up behind him was faster.

"Go, Sera!" Nur shouted.

The fire sprawled upwards into the shape of a person, and I could almost see a wicked smile playing on its lips before it slithered up the Icis' legs. The man screamed in shock, ceased summoning his cloud, and frantically patted the fire that had begun to spread all over his body.

The man flailed around helplessly, but the fire traveled, ever upwards, until it covered him from head to toe. He let out a series of ear-splitting shrieks as his skin sizzled and burned to a crisp.

I could smell his burnt flesh from where I hid and decided Nur and Seraphina clearly did *not* need my help, so I kept moving. The stench was just too unbearable to be around.

I picked up my pace, feeling more confident that I wouldn't be seen since the Icis didn't know to look above when I heard a struggle on my left. When I peered down, I noticed an Icis holding a sharpened icicle down over Aiden. With only a metal slab in the shape of a flame keeping the icicle from piercing his neck, Aiden needed help, and he needed it quick.

But, when I rushed down to action, the icicle slid off the edge of the slab and straight into Aiden's neck.

"*No!*" I yelled.

The Icis turned at the sound, and it was only then that I realized who stood before me. It was Laec, one of the brothers that had dropped me into the hole months ago, and I froze.

His eyes widened, filling with recognition and, as he watched the ground beneath me barrelling in his direction, he didn't attempt to counter me. Instead, he shouted my name at the top of his lungs, leaving me mystified as I watched my roots spear him over and over again.

Why would he yell my name with his last dying breath?

But I snapped out of it when I heard Aiden sputtering on the ground. I waited until Laec went limp, held up only by my roots, before rushing to Aiden's aide.

He lay gasping for air on the ground behind Laec's hole-ridden body. I knelt down at his side, placing my hands over the gushing wound, trying frantically to stop the bleeding. I grew yarrow on command and yanked the leaves off, padding them over the injury, but I could feel the pressure building at my palm, the blood begging to be let out.

Aiden watched me, clutching at my arms in desperation, his eyes crazy. Then, he lifts a hand, and a flame emerges from his palm only to transform to steel during a high flicker. Now, what Aiden held in his palm was no longer a flame but a steel blade, and he nudged it towards me with what remaining force he could muster.

Aiden made me a weapon.

I gave him a tiny, quiet "thank you," only realizing I had begun to cry when I could barely see his face through my tears.

His coughing subsided until it stopped altogether, and his black eyes became still and vacant.

"I'm sorry. I'm so sorry," I whispered, brushing Aiden's hair out of his face, but I couldn't stay here. I held onto the blade and sprinted out of the scene, remembering Laec's final call for help.

I weaved through the trees only to notice an Ignis with a strikingly long braid being chased by an Icis on my right. She ran like a chicken without a head—bearing a laceration from the base of her chest down to her belly.

I strafed to the right and focused my thoughts on growing a honey locust tree directly ahead of the Icis to throw him off balance and perhaps even put him out of commission when he collided against its thorns. But, unfortunately, my focus on the locust tree kept me from seeing the Icis that stood right before me.

I only saw a glimpse of her before a mist cloud obscured my vision and crept its way towards me. I turned to run only to see Kai falling to the ground behind me, gasping for air in a rolling sphere of water.

I looked in every direction, but the mist had reached me, cutting off my vision. I couldn't see anything past it. The fog clung to my skin and filled my lungs, making it difficult to breathe. I summoned a root, but I had nowhere to aim. I couldn't *see*.

Then, just as I heard the Icis sprinting in my direction, I caught another pair of footsteps as well. I braced myself for the impact, ready to slash the steel blade Aiden gifted me across the Icis, but I heard a crash a few feet ahead of me instead.

The fog disappeared to reveal the Icis laying on the ground with Eika's jaws savagely latched onto her throat.

"Thanks, baby," I whispered to her.

Eika's green eyes glowed as she thrashed the Icis around to get a better hold on her neck.

I turned, remembering there had been an Icis behind me, only to see Hestia's colossal bear tearing through him, but not in time to save Kai, who lay beside her, unresponsive.

I tensed when I didn't see Hestia anywhere near us. "Where is she?" I asked the bear, assuming she could answer me.

The bear placed her heavy paw over the Icis' chest, and I winced at the sound of his ribs cracking before she raised her head towards me. But, obviously, she didn't respond.

I lifted myself up a cottonwood in the hopes that I could spot Hestia over the canopy, but with no way to spot anything in the steam burgeoning overhead, I gave up.

I reminded myself that her ethos didn't require her to be in the animal's vicinity to influence them. I took solace in that.

A series of thunderous cracks and snaps emitted by a blazing Sitka Spruce filled the air. She had fallen victim to the fire raging around her, her needles having long since tapered off, leaving her branches bare, and now she had lost her grip on the earth and began her descent. Beneath her, an Ignis and Icis fought, oblivious to her demise until she collapsed right on top of them.

Three lives taken in the span of thirty seconds . . . We're way in over our heads.

I slumped against my cottonwood, gripping the ridges of her bark—exhausted. I planned on catching my breath only to see Fintan, of all people, powering up a fireball behind one of my willows, sweating profusely, while the Icis he fought appeared set with her power.

I contemplated leaving him to his own devices. Karma didn't always happen on its own—sometimes, it needed a little push. But as I turned to go, Nur's words came to mind.

As much as I detested Fintan, I couldn't turn a blind eye. He was an Ignis fighting for our cause. He was buffering the blow of the Icis, and I couldn't even recall how many of our people I had witnessed die by now, so I sighed and turned back.

I had a few seconds to jump, and I used it. I crawled onto the edge of my branch and dropped down between them with an unexpected splash. It seemed the Icis had inundated the woods, turning it almost swamp-like.

As soon as my feet touched the earth, I summoned a root out of the ground. It rose like a bullet from a gun, piercing her head and drenching me as if I had popped a blood-filled balloon.

We stood there together with our hands on our knees, panting. I turned to check on Fintan only to see him wide-eyed as he took in my bloody appearance. He didn't thank me, but he would do well to remember that moment.

Just as I went to resume my position in the protective canopy, I caught the foul stench of a crushed false azalea and stopped dead. I turned, and my blood ran cold when my eyes were pulled to the figure standing before me.

It was Nerio, the man that had starred in my night-mares every night since I first laid eyes on him. My entire body stiffened, and the hairs on the back of my neck rose.

He spits on the ground between us, a cruel smile forming on his face.

As soon as he began to raise his palms, I spun towards

Fintan for help, and sure enough, he wasn't there. Fuck. I sprinted in that direction anyway, hoping I'd run into him, Eika, or who I had longed to find this entire time—Levi.

This was the one person I could not fight—the person whose very name made my skin crawl. In his presence, every ounce of progress I had made over the last couple of months vanished, leaving me back to square one. And I could hear him hurtling towards me. My heart pounded madly as I sensed him catching up to me.

Think, Valerie . . . think . . .

I made an abrupt turn behind an aspen whose roots protruded from the ground, knowing it would slow me down some but hopeful it would slow him down more and possibly throw him off balance.

It didn't. And now Nerio was closer, still. I couldn't concentrate enough to set any intricate traps, so I gathered every ounce of strength I could muster and propelled myself further, desperate to stay out of range of his perverse ethos.

Because if Nerio closed the distance between us, I knew it would mean the end for me.

CHAPTER EIGHTEEN

PAPER TIGER

EREN

I was forced to stand since they reserved every makeshift seat for the elderly and pregnant Ignis. There were more of them underneath the floorboards, hiding like roaches in Hestia's secret bunker. A bunker Valerie had so conveniently hidden from me until yesterday when I could do nothing about it. Could Levi have relayed his suspicions to her?

No. Valerie would've, without a doubt, confronted me if he had.

Remembering Valerie's gifts, I pulled out the Airheads and the tiny magic eight ball from my pocket. I handed the candy to a kid trembling in the corner, and his mother gave me an appreciative nod. Though I did so to keep the candy from weighing me down and not because I remotely cared about her kid, I accepted her thanks. I could've just as easily thrown it away.

I peered down at the ball, rubbing my thumb over the

window to the die. I considered asking it a question, only to stuff it back into my pocket when I realized I didn't really want to know the answer to it. Not to mention, it would be juvenile to suggest a toy had any real way of predicting the future. And, despite what Valerie implied with giving me such inane gifts, I wasn't a child anymore.

The demons prayed and comforted each other—all in vain. Under no circumstances could the Ignis conceivably win against the Icis. They lacked discipline; they lacked commitment. Traits that the Icis bore ten-fold. But if I didn't provide the Icis with at least a morsel of information when they arrived, they'd assume I flipped, so I stepped around the Ignis until I reached the door.

"Where do you think you're going?" a heavyset woman asked. I recognized her as one of the Ignis' kitchen matrons.

"I forgot to mention something to Nur," I said.

"We were ordered to stay inside. No exceptions," a bearded Ignis added.

"It'll only take a minute," I muttered, tired of explaining myself to these insignificant people. I pried the door open and wiggled my way out before closing it behind me.

I had no intention of seeing Nur. Or anyone on this side of the war, for that matter. I intended to find the Icis before the Ignis did. I needed to warn them of the traps lying in wait for them before they took their frustrations out on Grant. Or on me.

I surveyed the area and immediately rounded the corner of the cabin when I saw Valerie and Cora interacting only a few feet away.

I stood there for a moment to be sure I hadn't been seen and then proceeded to run into the woods ahead, laying low. I couldn't think of a valid excuse for why I violated Nur's orders if I were to be caught, so I couldn't afford to.

AN HOUR PASSED AS I LURCHED DEEPER INTO THE WOODS, seeking to reach the fringes and catch the Icis just when they arrived. Then, the sound of a crashing wave broke through the silence.

The war had begun. I was too late.

I couldn't be caught like this by either faction; it would be too suspicious. So I searched for a tree to climb and found a giant one up ahead with thick drooping branches —perfect. But as I approached it, I recognized a plant at its base. A manchineel that Valerie had raved about only weeks ago.

See, the tree was deceptive. It promised shelter and safety, but there was no way around the manchineel if you wanted to reach the branches of the tree. And a simple touch of the milky sap on the manchineel's leaves or bark caused the skin to blister and burn. If introduced into the bloodstream, it could kill.

Valerie wanted an Icis to believe they could climb it. She wanted them to brush up against the plant on their way to safety only to succumb to its poison.

I ripped giant leaves off another plant, placed them over the manchineel to use as a buffer, and stepped over them onto the closest hanging branch. Once above ground, I brushed the buffer leaves away with my foot to hide the evidence and then continued to climb until I reached the top.

I was about twenty feet above the ground, and I couldn't have asked for a better hideout. I could see the tops of trees all around me and had a full view of a large clearing just a few yards away. I would hide away here until the coast was clear.

THE WAR WAS DEAFENING TO MY SENSITIVE EARS. BETWEEN the crashing of waves and the roaring fires, I tried to focus only on the sounds closest to me. As much as I would've liked to cover my ears or leave the field altogether, I couldn't. I needed to find a way to help the Icis in whatever way I could.

When I closed my eyes to weed out the sounds, I caught a familiar voice, and my eyes shot open. It was Levi, and he was close.

I pried myself up as I looked around and, finally, I saw him. He stood smack in the middle of the clearing, blue fires raging all around him. I watched in horror as Icis after Icis entered the field, confident in their ability to stop him since he was only one man. I could hear them coming, crashing through the woods.

But Levi breezed through them with ease, barely moving from where he stood. No matter what the Icis threw at Levi, he seemed to have inimitable stamina; his fires never receded.

The Icis dropped like flies around him, writhing in agony on the ground as his flames consumed them, leaving nothing but a shadow of who they once were etched into the ground.

At one point, three Icis stormed into the clearing all at once, and I thought they might actually stand a chance. But Levi *exploded*—his blue flames consuming his entire frame.

The three were blown to smithereens in the blast, but a

fourth I hadn't noticed leapt towards him, a giant orb of water levitating over his outstretched hands.

He smashed the ball over Levi, but instead of extinguishing him, the water instantly evaporated when it came in contact with his flames. But, of course, the Icis did not expect that, and now he was in close quarters with the devil.

The Icis turned on his heel, only to find a moose running to him at full speed, blocking his path. The Icis tried to side-step it, but the moose herded him back to where Levi stood. The Icis backed away from the mooses' thrashing antlers and turned to run in the opposite direction, only for Levi to bash his fiery fist into the Icis' face when he did.

The Icis collapsed. Before the blue flames spread over his body, I noticed the fist-shaped impression caved into his face where Levi's fist had landed, and I shuddered.

Calder did not prepare for this. He had based his plans on the actions of the twelve-year-old Levi's abilities. But this wasn't the same little boy.

This was a man without a pang of conscience. A man that had no scruples with killing and killing viciously. Levi showed no mercy or humanity, only ingenuity, in the way he ended their lives.

And where the hell did the moose come from?

Just as I thought Levi's reign of terror had finally ended, a figure entered the clearing. Calder.

Finally, s*omeone has to stop him . . .*

"Levi, the hell-raiser!" Calder called out as he traversed the clearing. "My oh my, how you've grown."

Levi's flame engulfed figure turned to him. "Have we met?"

"You wouldn't remember, but I came to visit when I heard the news of your birth. I had Udiya promise never to release you, but, as you well know, she was a stubborn woman. She never listened."

There was a long pause while Levi processed Calder's words.

Then, it dawned on me. The lock of black Ignis hair, the children's teeth . . . they weren't Calder's trophies as I had previously suspected—they were mementos. Calder had kept them as keepsakes to remember him by. They were Levi's.

"I heard through the grapevine you appointed a low-tier Ignis to take your place as their authority," Calder continued. "Nur, is it?"

Levi took a menacing step in his direction. "Keep his name out of your filthy mouth."

Calder laughed.

"He's more clever than all of you," Levi said. "Nur befriended the monster *you* created."

Calder gave a dismissive wave of his hand. "Fire is the devil's only friend, but you'll learn that soon enough, my son."

"Don't call me that," Levi hissed. "You abandoned her! You left her to deal with the shame and the fear for all those years—*alone*. You may have impregnated my mother, but I refuse to claim you as anything other than a hypocrite and a tyrant."

"Udiya never—"

"No," Levi interrupted. "Only a coward and a sorry excuse for a man would do what you've done. I don't want to hear your excuses. You're nothing more than a stranger to me, and when I kill you, and I promise you that I will, I'll feel nothing but *relief*. So, if you expected a happy reunion, prepare to be disappointed because I won't give you one."

I heard footsteps underneath my tree and caught Nerio

creeping past. "Psst," I called out to him, and he looked up at me. "Stay there. And don't touch those plants," I added, pointing towards the machineels.

Nerio nodded, and I focused my attention back on the two in the clearing.

"It pains me to hear your callous words," Calder said, "because I never intended to kill you, Levi. I understood my attachment to your mother was what led to your creation, so I was gracious enough to allow you to live your life in that cave with the rest of the vermin, only for you to go and evoke that girl. A foolish decision on its own, but then to add insult to injury, you had your pets take Pavati, forcing my hand. You've only done this to yourself."

I wished I could see Levi's expression, but it remained shrouded underneath his flames.

"Where is she, Levi?" Calder asked.

"Where's Grant?" Levi asked in return.

"You take a great deal of interest in that Natura's affairs. Now, why is that?"

Levi didn't answer, but I heard a scream coming from a different part of the woods.

Someone yelled my sister's name.

I motioned to Nerio below and pointed in the direction of the scream. "Valerie's down that way," I whispered. "*Hurry*."

Nerio bolted in the direction I pointed, leaving me alone once again.

"No matter," Calder muttered to Levi. "It will make no difference tomorrow when all of this nonsense is behind us. It's time for a new beginning."

"I think history will see things differently," Levi said as he lifted his arms, charging his fire.

Only Calder did the same. He hurled water overhead,

solidified them to steel as they peaked, and launched the shards at Levi.

But Levi was two steps ahead and dodged the spears before sending a blue fireball streaking in his direction. Calder succeeded in generating a steel wall ahead of him, albeit by the skin of his teeth, each firing a flurry of attacks while the other did everything in their power to evade them. They were neck and neck until two figures bounded through the woods and into the clearing.

It was Valerie, with Nerio on her tail, and she appeared to be holding a stake.

As relieved as I was that he managed to find her, I was less than enthused that he hadn't dealt with her in the woods. I knew what I did was right, but I still didn't want to watch her death unfold before me. Even I had my limits.

A surge of Nerio's acid hit Valerie's back, knocking her off her feet and the stake from her hands. She grunted at the impact, scrambling away from Nerio as he advanced.

"No, no, no!" she cried.

Levi's head snapped towards the sound of her voice, distracting him from the spear Calder had sent hurtling in his direction, and Levi staggered when it grazed his shoulder.

Nerio stood above Valerie now, kicking past what little foliage she managed to call to her aid so he could maintain a steady flow of acid cascading over her.

She shielded her face with her arms, but by the sound of her cries, acid still found a way through.

That sick bastard!

Calder promised he'd dispose of her quickly and pain-lessly, but there was Nerio, torturing Valerie for his own sick amusement.

"Stop!" Levi's figure roared towards Nerio. "Fight *me*!"

The pain in Levi's voice confirmed my suspicions. His

focus became divided between his fight against Calder and his instinct to save my sister, but Levi fought the urge to run to her, knowing it would only benefit Calder if he turned his back to him. This fight turned out to be more than a mere survival of the fittest; this was psychological warfare.

Calder, though visibly winded, chuckled at Levi's reaction. "Do it, boy, and I'll end you."

Levi growled in frustration, his head whipping wildly between Valerie's struggle and the murderous man before him. He was between the devil and the deep blue sea, and he knew it.

But, when another agonizing scream tore through Valerie's throat, Levi's entire frame shook as though it could no longer contain his anguish until the man exploded for yet a *second* time. He let out a tormented battle cry and charged in Calder's direction.

Calder scrambled to defend himself, fully encasing himself in his steel, but that did nothing to deter the now enraged Levi, who leaped onto the casing with ease. He smashed his fire engulfed fist against a single spot over and over again until his fire melted through.

As the steel gave way, a spear Calder prepared in the meantime shot out, but Levi wasn't stupid enough to peer into the opening. He distanced himself from the hole as the spear emerged, avoiding it altogether. Then, he torched the inside of the casing, reducing his father to a pile of ashes in the process.

Calder didn't scream when he died.

Levi hopped off the casing, still completely covered in flames, and raced towards Nerio.

Nerio panicked at the sight of Levi's form bounding towards him. He looked down at Valerie's writhing body, trying to decide whether to risk his life by touching her or settle for whatever Levi had in store for him. His head turned to the stake Valerie dropped earlier, and he picked it up, threw himself on top of her, and plunged the steel straight into her abdomen.

An explosion erupted in the west, and though she had just been stabbed, Valerie's full attention focused on the sound. Valerie pushed Nerio's face away with her hands, and his cheeks caved as she drained the life right out of him.

When Levi finally reached them, he removed his fire and flung Nerio's limp and shriveled body off of Valerie.

Valerie's screams changed after the explosion. They were guttural and raw, now. She fought to bring herself back to her feet, clutching at her stomach, but couldn't muster the strength to do so.

Levi attempted to soothe her, but he, too, was frantic as he took in her wound. Finally, he settled on lifting her and cradled her to his chest, running in the direction of the cabin.

I took a moment to process what I had just witnessed.

Calder was dead, and so was the only person capable of getting a jump on Valerie. I could only hope Valerie's wound proved fatal, but I trembled all over.

Levi survived. And he knew my role in this. Perhaps if he would've succumbed to Calder's attacks, then I would've had a chance, but now? I was on my own.

I scrambled out of the tree, hoping to find the keys to the Jeep and make a run for it, when I came face to face with Valerie's panther.

"Shh," I whispered, backing away slowly when I saw her blood-sodden mouth.

She hissed at me, her eyes oozing with hostility, and I sprinted in the opposite direction in response, never having ran so fast in my entire life.

CHAPTER NINETEEN
DEAD AS A DODO

VALERIE

By the time I regained consciousness, I was drenched in sweat and gasping for air. All around me, the non-fighting Ignis watched as Ren worked to stop the bleeding, but as soon as she noticed I had woken up, she paused.

"It's just me, Valerie! Don't drain me," Ren said, her hands held high.

I nodded, gritting my teeth against the constant throbbing in my abdomen. The adrenaline that had once kept the pain at bay had worn off. Now, I couldn't move an inch without the original stabbing sensation returning for an encore.

Ren placed her hands on me again, pressing down on my stomach with her blood-stained hands. Fortunately, it didn't look like any of it belonged to her.

I cried out in pain and only a moment later felt hands in my hair. Levi peered down at me, eyes wide and anxious.

"I'm sorry," I whispered to him, catching a glimpse of the wound on his shoulder. It wouldn't have happened if it weren't for me. If I would've just dealt with Nerio on my own instead of running to Levi like some defenseless puppy. Ugh, how *pathetic*.

"What?" he asked. "You have nothing to be sorry for."

I was about to elaborate when a needle pierced my skin, making me groan.

"I have to sew this up now," Ren said. "Stop squirming."

I shouted profanities while Levi held me down, wondering why the hell she didn't think to numb the area first. The meticulous technique Ren opted for had me raging, and I pounded my clenched fist against the mattress in tandem with Ren's punctures to distract myself.

Does she think she's knitting a fucking scarf? Get on with it!

At last, Ren finished, but the wound continued to throb.

"Now, I can work," she sighed, and, almost instantly, I felt a surge of something, something I couldn't quite place. A liquid coursed through me, washing away the pain and leaving behind only a tiny sliver of what it once was.

"Count yourself lucky it didn't pierce any organs," Ren said. "Incredibly lucky. You'll be fine so long as you limit your movements. Otherwise, you'll tear the stitches."

"Did we win?" I asked, perching myself up on my elbows as I scanned the crowd. If Levi was here with me and not out there, then that must mean we won. But if we had, I couldn't tell by the expression on the faces of those around me.

Levi's eyes flickered to mine only to revert back to examining Ren's stitches before answering. "You could say that."

"Eren?" I called out into the crowd.

"He's outside. He's fine," Levi said, his voice terse.

"Did they find Grant? Where's Cora and Hestia?"

Levi didn't look up now, unnaturally invested in the pattern of the stitching.

I swatted his hand away, scrambled out of bed, and headed for the door.

Levi followed. "What the hell did Ren just say to you?"

Though each stride pulled at the edges of my wound, I didn't stop. I needed to find my brothers. I needed to find Cora.

THE SIGHT OF THE IGNIS DRAGGING THE DEAD BACK TO THE cabin greeted me, and I was not at all prepared for what I saw. Time stood still as my mind wrestled between sifting through the bodies and running back into the cabin to break away from all the misery. But the first took over, and I examined each face, growing more and more discouraged as I went.

I peered over a hunched-over Ignis, and my hand flew over my mouth as I held in a gag.

Not because I knew the deceased, though I did—not personally, anyway—but because the man happened to be stuffing the dead woman's innards back into her belly. The belly of the girl with the strikingly long braid that I had so tragically failed to save.

The man paused to wipe the sweat from his brow, only to inadvertently smear her blood across his face in the process.

I turned away from the gruesome scene and focused on the bodies already lined up by the fire. I recognized Kai, the Ignis crushed by the falling tree, and Aiden . . . kind, noble Aiden.

Regrettably, I wasn't the only one to spot him.

Off to the side, Seraphina sat catatonic on a boulder, gaping at the state of her former lover. Fintan, his hands on either side of her face, strove to console her, but she was so distraught over the loss that I doubt she could even hear his words while so stupefied.

I didn't know what to do. I only found more suffering and death everywhere I looked, but one thing was abundantly clear.

We did not win this war. Winning doesn't look like this. The more I saw, the less I thought we'd ever recover.

"Valerie, please. Come back inside. You're injured," Levi insisted, tugging on my arm.

I brushed him off, dreading to find my worst nightmare in the hoard of the dead before me, and sighed in relief when I didn't find it.

Someone's hand grazed my hair, and I turned to see Zoran. Soiled, sweaty, and spent.

"Hey," I breathed, and though he didn't respond, he gave me a sad smile before returning to his work, gathering the departed.

One down, six to go, I thought, scanning the campsite for the others.

"If you're looking for Hestia, she's off sending word to the Natura of the outcome," Levi said.

"Oh, thank you," I sighed, only to stop in my tracks as I rounded the cabin.

Levi cursed under his breath and attempted to pull me away, but my feet were nailed to the ground. I couldn't move, even if I wanted to.

This was the site of the explosion I heard earlier. I could see the blast zone right before me. Flesh and bone scattered around a person that looked awfully familiar.

The body lay twisted inhumanly, its spine bent. Their

black eyes bulged out of their sockets, their mouth hung open, and their now deep indigo veins jutted out almost an inch above their skin as blood oozed out of every orifice.

I approached carefully, only for my knees to buckle out from under me.

Levi stepped forward, placing one hand under the woman's chin and the other over her head, before snapping her mouth shut, and I flinched at the sound it made.

I motioned towards a small arm strewn on the grass next to her. "Fiametta?" I asked.

And, though I couldn't be sure I even asked it aloud, Levi nodded.

My eyes returned to the body before me. Although this person looked like her, my mind couldn't fathom the idea that it belonged to her—to my friend. It had to belong to someone else . . . this couldn't be my Cora.

I glanced down, catching the shimmer of her silver bracelet as the sun reflected off of it. I carefully unclasped it from her wrist only to notice the hand clutched something else, and when I pried her fingers open, a small black ball fell to the ground.

I grabbed the magic eight ball, forming a tight fist around it.

"Come, Valerie. You need to rest," Levi whispered.

Cora's beautiful black hair dangled over her ashen face. I brushed the strands away, allowing my fingers to linger there. "Iri?"

"She survived."

"Could you bring her to me?"

I yearned to comfort her, to show her she wasn't alone, but Iri couldn't remember her sisters this way. I couldn't allow the image that I was so sure would haunt me forever to haunt her too. No matter what Cora meant to me, her sisters meant *everything* to her. She wouldn't want Iri to see her like this.

So, when Levi left to fetch her, I transformed the gruesome scene before me.

My vines took special care as they laid Cora onto her back, wrapping themselves around her and the few intact parts of Fiametta, welcoming them back to the earth from which they came.

I wished I could've had more time with Cora, if only to ask what her favorite flower was. But time wasn't on our side, so I had to settle for all of them in the hopes that maybe her favorite would be among them.

Soon, milkweeds, trilliums, jessamines, wisterias, violets, and every other flower I could think of covered every inch of death previously imprinted on the ground. In this now lush and fecund garden, no one would ever know the atrocities that transpired here.

I heard Iri's sobs before I saw her.

Her cries shook her petite frame as tears rolled down her face, and she threw herself against me instantly, clinging to me as if to keep from falling apart.

Though hopeless, I stroked her hair to comfort her. "I'm sorry," I whispered over and over again into her hair.

What else could I say? I was just as much to blame for her sister's death as the Icis who struck the killing blow because when it came time to act, I choked. How could I agree to help Cora when I couldn't even help myself?

There was nothing I could do for my friend now but watch over and protect her surviving sister. I wouldn't— *couldn't*—let her down again.

"We found one!" someone yelled behind us.

Levi helped me up as I struggled to my feet. I sought to carry Iri, but Levi scooped her up instead while we made our way to the group. As much as I wanted to crumble onto the ground and weep, it would need to wait. I had to find my brothers still.

I rallied what energy remained and trudged along until I saw the cause of all the commotion. Two men had emerged from the woods. A tall Icis, with a scar across his throat, scanned the crowd as he held up another mutilated man, who could barely keep his dark, crusted head up, let alone his eyes.

I recognized the man with the scar immediately. It was Salil—Laec's brother, but he donned a new, fresh wound now. Half of his body appeared burned, as though he'd been in close proximity to an explosion. And the fury that consumed me when I realized why nearly blinded me.

"It was you . . ." I began, taking an automatic step in his direction as the image of Cora's grotesque corpse flashed before me. And, Fiametta…a child with nothing left to identify her by except for teeth. The deep breath I took did nothing to reign in my rage.

"Valerie," Nur cautioned, positioning himself between us. "Let me handle this."

The man Salil held up reanimated at the name. "Valerie . . . ? Is that you?"

I watched in horror as the man lifted his head only to notice his green eyes, *my* green eyes, staring back at me. Grant stood before me, mangled in blood and dirt almost beyond recognition.

"Oh my god!" I yelled, scrambling to him only for Salil to tighten his grip on the back of his neck, making Grant wince.

Levi held me back, but I thrashed against him. "Let go of him!"

Grant began to weep, his entire face twisting into one of anguish. "Why are they doing this to me, Val? *Please.* Please, help me," he cried.

A strange sound escaped my throat, and I held my breath. I could feel my heart racing, but I needed to maintain my composure if Grant was to survive this. "What do you want, Salil?"

"We've got someone he might want," Nur said, locking eyes with Seraphina and motioning towards the cabin. "Get Pavati."

Salil laughed, blood dripping from the corner of his mouth. "I don't give a fuck about *Pavati*," he said to Nur, though his eyes never strayed from mine. "You could skin that vapid whore alive for all I care."

"Oh, we just might," Seraphina said, ignoring Nur's warning glare. "But, if you don't let him go, we'll be sure to practice on you first."

Though Salil didn't say a word, his anger had him all but foaming at the mouth.

"Just tell me what you want, Salil, and I'll give it to you," I pleaded. "What do you want?"

"Take a wild fucking guess, *half-breed*," he spat, blood gushing out of his mouth and nearly reaching my feet. "You've massacred my people, butchered my brother! There's nothing left for me to want . . . Nothing left but *this*. This is for Laec," he said, his expression one of sorrow as he said the name, and then a terrible scream erupted from Grant's throat only to be cut off by a gurgle. "An eye for an eye," Salil breathed, falling to the ground next to my brother's now seizing body.

"Oh my god," I gasped, rushing to lift Grant's head off the ground. I grew yarrow as I watched the blood seep from his eyes, his ears, his nose, trying desperately to stop whatever had a hold on him, but I couldn't find the source.

Where the fuck is the source?

Levi rushed forward, prying Grant's mouth open and

shoveling out the massive clumps of blood that had begun to obstruct his breathing, only for more to take its place.

"His organs," Levi said. "They're rupturing. Ren!"

Ren parted the crowd and hurried to Grant, placing her hands on his chest.

"Well, if it isn't the traitorous bitch," Salil hissed. "Turning your back on your people and your sex . . . You make me *sick*."

Ren glanced at him fleetingly before focusing her attention back on Grant. She squeezed her eyes shut, straining to do whatever it was she did, only to shake her head in frustration. "I'm sorry, Valerie. There's nothing I can do."

"No! Try harder," I demanded.

But, Grant's seizing worsened, and he sputtered wildly between my hands. His skin paled, and his eyes bulged. Ren grunted as she pushed her ethos to its limit, only for Grant to become still—*unnervingly* still.

"Ren, please," I breathed. "Help him!"

"He's too far gone," Ren whispered. "I'm sorry. He's gone."

I held Grant, gaping at his ruptured face, unable to accept her words. He was so close, right here in my arms—only now, dead.

As time chipped away, so did my shock, leaving the earth and me shaking with a fury I could no longer contain. The earth itself feeling my grief, my pain. How had it come to this?

I turned to the sound of the others screaming and caught Salil staring daggers at Eren while Eren's sobbing figure stumbled to get away from him.

And I saw red, whispering, "Don't even fucking think about it," before I hit the button.

The button opened every latch inside of me, freeing my ethos' fragments from their cells and leaving them to do their worst. I could only vaguely hear the others over the rushing blood in my ears before I had the earth swallow Salil whole.

My vines wrapped around his massive, muscular body, but no matter how hard he fought, he was no match for them. Salil screamed and cursed, wrestling and wailing against the vines, and when he saw that it didn't faze me, he resorted to begging, utterly unaware that nothing he said or did could save him now. Nothing could undo what he'd done.

As the sound of Salil's bones shattering into a thousand pieces filled the air, I dragged my finger across my throat and watched as his eyes widened in response.

I reveled in his torment for a moment longer before I had the earth crush him, pulverizing him like worthless trash sent through a compactor.

Chapter Twenty

RED HERRING

EREN

I waited for the band of Ignis hovering around the cabin to leave before I stepped out of the woods, only to see Levi and Nur waiting for me when I did, and I couldn't hold it in any longer. The truth gusted out of me like smoke from a blown gasket.

There was no point in omitting what I knew. There was no escaping it now.

Levi's expression remained detached as he listened, though occasionally, I'd notice a muscle in his jaw twitch.

Nur, on the other hand, was visibly incensed, recalling the past year where the Ignis had gone above and beyond for me.

But the Ignis were just as culpable as I was, maybe even more so. They turned their backs on their kind, leaving me to make the unpopular decision, leaving me with no choice. It wasn't an easy choice to make, but I was strong enough to make it. One day, they would thank me, but today was not that day . . .

Valerie's cries sent Levi rushing into the cabin, and Nur paused his seething to help Fintan drag Aiden's limp corpse back to camp. With the heat taken off me, I was left to brood over my predicament by the blown-out campfire alone.

I was furious with the Icis for allowing their egos to blind them from reality. Had Nerio not spent so long enjoying the sight of Valerie thrashing on the ground, then he would have had ample time to kill her. And had Calder not considered himself untouchable and taken Levi more seriously, then he would have had a chance to kill him as well. It seemed the only person who managed to hold up their end of the bargain was the measly little Ventus.

And then, only ten minutes later, Salil sealed his fate, and all hell broke loose.

"Get. Her. Out. *Now*," Nur barked at Levi.

My ears rang in the aftershock. I could hardly see through my rage after watching Salil murder Grant, and I knew if Valerie hadn't killed him, I would've done so myself with my own bare hands. How could he do this to me after everything I had done for them?

"What the hell just happened?" Seraphina mumbled.

Valerie looked shell-shocked as she stared at Grant's body until she heard my sobs and took steps in my direction, only for Levi to hold her back.

"Don't go to the well," he said. "There's no water there."

"What?"

He rubbed his brow, his expression strained.

"What do you mean, Levi?" Valerie asked.

I froze. *Shit.* I needed to get my two cents in before Levi painted me into some sort of monster. I didn't feel even an ounce of remorse, but if I didn't make a case for myself, then I was undoubtedly a dead man.

It was the first time I had seen Valerie in action, and it only validated my beliefs, wiping away every uncertainty I might've still harbored. I knew then that everything I had done up until that point, Valerie more than merited. She was too powerful, too unpredictable. She couldn't be policed if she could have the ground gobble you up on a whim.

"You have to understand," I said, my words coming out in a rush, "it wasn't supposed to happen like this. I was in too deep. I had no choice but to see it through!"

Valerie pushed against Levi to comfort me, but he just wouldn't budge.

"I've looked back at everything that's gone wrong, and he's the only common thread," Levi said to her.

She looked at him in confusion, not understanding what he meant. All she wanted to do was run to me as I wept pathetically on the ground.

"He conspired with the Icis from the very beginning, Valerie," Nur said.

Hearing those words . . . my heart went into freefall. The shoe dropped, and my soul nearly left my body.

It was one thing for Nur and Levi to know, but I hadn't prepared myself for this. I hadn't prepared myself to see Valerie's reaction to my betrayal. I assumed she'd be killed before anyone could tell her and be none the wiser.

"You conniving piece of shit," Seraphina hissed at me.

Valerie shook her head, blinking rapidly. "Don't be ridiculous. That's not true."

"It's true," Levi whispered.

"No! You're wrong!" she yelled and freed herself with a

vicious yank. She rushed to me, but I couldn't stop myself from recoiling; I couldn't bear to have her hands on me.

"Get away from me!" I shouted, eyes burning with an animosity I no longer had to suppress. "I'm not a kid anymore, Valerie. I can fend for myself. I had a plan . . . The Icis promised me they'd let him go, but then you had to go and kill Laec, pushing Salil to get even. You killed him. Grant's death is on *you*."

And, without thinking it through, I dove towards her.

Valerie was in such a state of shock that she didn't think to stop or drain me, so I pushed her to the ground. But, just as I reached for her throat, Levi pulled me off and flung me to the side, the impact knocking the air right out of me.

He flattened me against a tree by my throat. "I can't let you do that, Eren."

Though Levi's expression remained impassive, I knew better. He had been waiting for this moment for weeks, the chance to be rid of me. The chance to drain me, at last. I had no idea what it would feel like to have all the water withdrawn from my system, but I was sure it would be excruciating, so I shut my eyes and braced myself . . . and, nothing.

I waited a moment longer, but still, nothing happened. I opened my eyes slowly and saw a vine wrapped around Levi's wrist.

"Don't touch him," Valerie said, clutching at her belly where blood had begun to seep through. Roots rose from the ground, pointing in every direction, daring anyone to defy her. "I—I can't think," she stammered. "I can't...deal with this right now. Not when Grant . . . God, I can't even say it. *Please*, Levi. I can't lose Eren, too. There has to be some sort of misunderstanding."

I looked into Levi's cold eyes before he mastered his ire

and stepped back, releasing his hold on me when he noticed the fresh blood leaching through Valerie's shirt.

Nur backed away from me, following Levi's lead reluctantly, but Seraphina took Levi's place, pinning me to the tree.

"I swear to fucking god, Seraphina," Valerie said. "I get that we've both lost people today, but if you don't take your hands off him, you'll live to regret it."

Seraphina's tear-filled eyes darted from Nur to Valerie in rapid succession before puffing out her chest, and her grip on my arm only tightened. "I don't take orders from the likes of you."

Valerie's roots wrapped around her wrists, pulling her away from me while Seraphina fought against them, and then Ren jumped into the action.

"Stop!" Ren yelled. "Don't hurt her. If not for her sake, Valerie, then for mine."

Though Valerie had lost so much blood she could barely stand, she didn't take her eyes off Seraphina. She staggered to the right, but Levi caught her before she could fall.

"*Levi*. Do something," Nur urged.

Levi only averted his gaze. "Let go, Sera. Eren isn't foolish enough to try that again."

Seraphina scoffed but ultimately let go.

Nur regarded Levi with an inscrutable expression before pinching the bridge of his nose.

"Valerie," Nur began, "you killed this Icis without consulting us. If you had, then you would know that it does more harm than good to kill them. Now, his ethos will return to the cycle before we've even established where we stand. I need you to consult with me now. I need you to be sensible."

"What's one more Icis after the scores we've killed?" she asked. "None deserved to die as much as Salil."

"The war had already ended when you killed Salil. We needed him alive to garner what information we could, but now we'll never know what he knew."

"Why are you giving me shit over this? You already have Pavati!" Valerie yelled, quivering with so much aggravation that it sent a tremor through the earth.

Nur watched her measuredly, waiting for her to cool down.

"I'm . . . I'm sorry. My brain isn't quite firing on all cylinders yet," Valerie admitted.

Nur walked over to her and extended his hand, and though Seraphina and Fintan objected, he waved them away.

She eyed it warily before accepting it.

"You're in shock," Nur said. "We all are, so we understand. Everyone's trying to process what's happened, the people we've lost, but I need you to listen to me now."

Valerie nodded, a pitiful look in her eyes.

"Eren worked with the Icis. He told them of our plans, our numbers. He told them about you. I can't imagine how difficult it must be to hear that your own brother conspired against you, but Eren hasn't been your brother for a long time. The person you grew up with is gone, Valerie. That boy you see there," he said, pointing at me, "he's someone else. And, if it weren't for his actions, many of those we lost today would still be here…including Grant."

She shook her head in denial, crying, refusing to accept his words.

Nur squeezed her hand. "He's been evoked, so he will not be harmed. At least until we know what ethos he possesses. I can promise you that much. But we can't just let him ride off into the sunset, either."

"Evoked?" she managed to ask between her sobs. "But, how?"

"He said your mother helped evoke him."

"My mother's dead."

"She must've survived the crash somehow," Nur said. "Eren told us he had contact with her in Reota."

"That can't be . . ." she trailed off, wiping the snot that had pooled over her upper lip. "I mean, I saw my mom after the accident."

Levi's head snapped to her. "Are you sure?"

"Am I sure? Yes. Of course. The ceremony was open casket."

Levi had Zoran take his place holding Valerie up before turning to me with a wild look in his eyes. "You told us it was your mother."

"Don't look at me!" I cried, backing away from him. "I didn't know that because none of them ever spoke to me about her—ever. I know more about our neighbor than I do about my own mother. And why is everyone so hyper-fixated on me? Have any of you stopped to think about how Ren got to live here with you? Maybe she was spying for them all along, too!"

Ren, in a wave of uncharacteristic anger, rushed forward. "I am no traitor. You just placed your devotion on the wrong faction."

"You sided against your own people! You are, by definition—"

"Stop talking, Eren," Valerie snapped. "If you're not going to explain yourself, then just stop talking. Because listening to you try to scramble your way out of this hole you've dug yourself is just mortifying."

I turned to her in utter disbelief, and she returned my gaze with absolute abhorrence.

A hush drew across the campsite at Valerie's biting

words, but I couldn't understand how she had the gall to look so appalled.

"I had every right to help enforce my beliefs, Valerie," I said. "I deserve to feel like I can make a difference. I deserve to feel . . . significant. The spotlight doesn't always have to be on you."

"Our brother is dead, and that's all you can think about? You really are worse off than I thought."

I stood to face her, ready to finally unload the slew of trauma I had accumulated over the years by Valerie's own hand, only for Levi to shove me against the trunk of the tree again.

"Sit *down*," he demanded.

"Alright, I'm down!" I yelled, throwing my hands in the air. I massaged over the sore spot where the trunk scraped against the back of my head, but it did little to relieve the pounding ache.

"Now, tell me," Levi said, kneeling to meet me at eye level. "Why did you lie about seeing your mother in Reota, Eren?"

"Look, it was my mom. Okay? I mean, I couldn't see her, but it was her spirit."

"Her spirit?" he asked and paused for a moment to think it over. "A spirit," he repeated, and then, his entire body stiffened. "The Ventus' mimicry elemental."

Nur's eyes widened, and he placed a hand on Fintan's shoulder for support as terror thundered down on him.

"What does that mean?" Valerie asked Levi.

Seraphina answered instead, though her eyes remained fixed on me. "Every species has a mimicry ethos. The way I can mimic fire and Pavati can mimic water, there's a Ventus that can mimic air."

"That wasn't your mother, Eren," Levi said through clenched teeth. "That was a Ventus."

"But, I could swear—"

Levi pounded his fist against the tree a mere three inches from my head, and I flinched. "They played you, and you fell for it like the gullible fool that you are."

"But how could that be true?" I asked. "I *saw* her. I *spoke* with her. I specifically recall . . ."

And then it hit me. Every time I relayed my hesitations to Calder, I'd be sent to her, where her spirit would talk me down from the ledge. Every time I showed even the slightest reluctance . . .

How could Calder do this to me?

We stood like that for a while in an awful, trembling silence, attempting to grasp precisely what this meant for us, and I didn't dare move as I wrestled with a pain that nearly unmanned me. I could no longer tell the real from the fabricated. I could no longer tell what the point was for any of it.

Then, almost on cue, a fierce gust of wind tore through our camp. The gale flew so strong that it lifted debris, violently flinging leaves and twigs all around us.

Levi and Nur locked eyes for a moment before springing into action.

"*Run!*" Nur roared, frantically guiding everyone into the cabin.

Levi thrust Valerie into Zoran's arms, ordering him to take her inside.

"What's going on?" I asked Levi.

He didn't answer. Instead, he grabbed my arm and hauled me along with him towards the cabin.

It was chaos. Every Ignis took the body of a deceased with them as they darted inside, but Levi stopped by the door, noticing the three bodies that still remained out in the open.

"Grab one," Levi ordered as he lugged a body over his shoulder and dragged the other.

The remaining body, with its skin blistered and turned a greenish-black, no longer resembled a person. Their face was unrecognizable—a distended snarled mess. I eyed the bloated corpse in disgust, not sure where to even begin. Both his arms and legs looked as though they'd simply snap off if I tugged on them.

"Grab the damn body, Eren!"

I made a repulsed sound and went for the man's ankles. The feel of his swollen flesh as I secured my grip nearly made me hurl, so I held my breath, struggling against his weight as I pulled him into the cabin behind Levi. I dropped the body against the pile made by the others before Levi ushered me into an opening in the planks—the bunker.

Once everyone made their way inside, the old Natura woman slammed the hatch shut, leaving us all in complete darkness. We huddled together, hushing those who had naturally begun to panic until the overhead lighting began to flicker on and off above us, allowing us to see—even if it was only each other's frightened faces. The Ignis consoled their crying children until the only sound left was that of our shallow breathing. The stench of stale bodies and sweat in the bunkers' canned air made it difficult to breathe, but a disturbance above us captured my attention.

The Ventus had arrived at the scene, and I wasn't sure how much the Ignis could hear, but I heard it all.

"I see a copious amount of blood but not a single Ignis," a woman said, her voice dull and blank. "Could the Icis have been so outmatched?"

"I was told the impurities were very capable," another woman said, but this voice I *did* recognize. It belonged to the self-proclaimed "spirit" of my mother. "But I can't imagine they were capable enough to blow the Icis completely out of the water like this."

"What did you expect? This is what happens when you leave the work to such a mediocre and inept faction."

They continued to speak amongst themselves as they took in the war-torn landscape, and I drew in a large breath, only for Levi to slap a hand over my mouth.

"Not a sound," Levi hissed into my ear, knowing exactly where my mind had gone. "I don't even want to hear you breathe."

If he hadn't, I would've screamed bloody murder to alert the Ventus of our presence under the floorboards. But now, with Levi's hand clamped over my mouth, I was out of options. If even the slightest whimper escaped my lips, he'd drain me.

As desperately as I needed to escape and return to my people, this was not the time.

It was a bitter pill, but even though the Icis lost this battle, it did, in fact, bring me one step closer to reuniting with my faction. So perhaps this failure was essential to the bigger picture.

I would just need to impugn the allegations against me and prey on my sister's sympathies until I'm able to reunite with the Ventus because now, with Calder and Nerio gone, I was the only one with the power to end this.

My sister and the Ignis assumed I'd be easy to control because I wasn't blessed with a combat ethos, but that is not the case. What I lacked in physical strength, I made up for in willpower and total apathy. I had gone too far, lost too much to get here. It couldn't have been for nothing. This war had only proven that, though they may win, they couldn't do so without making severe sacrifices, and I could already see Valerie's mental health hanging on by a thread.

But, as much as they needed me, I needed them too.

The Ventus were my only hope to uncover the reason as to why I grew up without a mother, all while lost in my sister's twisted shadow.

And, with the Ventus by my side, I would not fail again.

The saga continues October 31, 2022 in
BURIED: THE ETHOS SERIES, BOOK TWO.

Made in United States
Orlando, FL
31 October 2021

10133865R00143